A M I L L I O N   W I N D O W S

GERALD MURNANE

A Million Windows

DAVID R. GODINE, PUBLISHER

FIRST US EDITION PUBLISHED IN 2016 BY
DAVID R. GODINE, PUBLISHER
POST OFFICE BOX 450
JAFFREY, NEW HAMPSHIRE 03452

FIRST PUBLISHED IN 2014
FROM THE WRITING & SOCIETY RESEARCH CENTRE
AT THE UNIVERSITY OF WESTERN SYDNEY
BY THE GIRAMONDO PUBLISHING COMPANY

DESIGNED BY HARRY WILLIAMSON
TYPESET BY ANDREW DAVIES
IN 10/17 PT BASKERVILLE

LIBRARY OF CONGRESS CATALOGING-IN-PUBLICATION
DATA

MURNANE, GERALD, 1939-
 A MILLION WINDOWS / GERALD MURNANE.
     PAGES ; CM
 ISBN 978-1-56792-555-5 (HARDCOVER : ACID-FREE
PAPER)
1. STORYTELLING--TECHNIQUE--FICTION.
2. INTERPERSONAL RELATIONS--FICTION.
3. AUTHORSHIP--FICTION. 4. TRUST--FICTION. I. TITLE.
 PR9619.3.M76M55 2015
 823'.914--DC23
2015024979

FIRST US EDITION, 2016
PRINTED IN THE UNITED STATES OF AMERICA

The house of fiction has in short not one window, but a million...

HENRY JAMES

The single holland blind in his room was still drawn down in late afternoon, although he would have got out of his bed and would have washed and dressed at first light. At the moment when he became a personage in this work of fiction, I supposed him to be seated at his small desk with his back to the glowing blind and to be reading, by the light of a desk-lamp, a sentence that he had written, perhaps only a few minutes earlier, at the head of a blank page. The sentence was his remembered version of a quotation, so to call it, that he had read long before. He recalls, or so I suppose, that the author of the sentence was a male person from an earlier century but he cannot recall the name of the author. The sentence is as follows: *All our troubles arise from our being unwilling to keep to our room.*

One of the commonest devices used by writers of fiction is the withholding of essential information. Much faulty fiction seems to derive from its author's having been overly influenced by films, and yet I have to admit that authors were withholding information from readers long before the first film-scripts were written. Long before cameras could record such scenes, solitary characters were reported as sitting in quiet rooms or trudging across lonely landscapes at the beginnings of works of fiction while the readers of those works looked forward to learning, all in good time, the names of those characters, their histories, and even their motives and deepest feelings. The narrator of *this* work of fiction wants no reader of the previous paragraph to look forward to learning any such details in connection with the personage mentioned there.

How many years have passed since I last watched a film – since I last walked out of some or other cinema ashamed at having wasted an afternoon or an evening and bothered already by the first of the clusters of false images that would occur to me again and again in coming weeks – false because their source was not my mind but sequences of shapes and colours displayed in the visible world as though objects and surfaces were all? And yet, when young I had hoped for much from films. I had hoped to see, in black-and-white scenery arranged by persons with mostly European names, visible, memorable signs from what I would have called, at that time, the world of imagination, as though it was a place I had yet to discover. One of the European names was a certain Swedish name, and that same name took my eye on the day before I began this work of fiction and while

I was turning the pages of a weekly news-magazine from some or another year in the 1980s. One of the pages was headed *CINEMA*, and I would have turned the page without reading it if the Swedish name had not taken my eye. I gathered from the little I read that the Swede, late in his career, had directed, if that is the correct word, a film set in a castle many a room of which was occupied by one or another chief character from one or another of the many films directed by the Swede in earlier years.

I read once that the writer of fiction Henry James got much enjoyment from hearing from fellow-guests at dinner-parties anecdotes that he later made use of in his fiction. James, however, as soon as he had decided that something he was hearing would later be of use to him, begged his informant not to go further; not to reveal the outcome of what was being recounted. At a certain point, James had seemingly got all the ingredients he needed for a work of fiction and preferred to devise his own outcome rather than merely report the actual. When I closed the pages of the weekly news-magazine as soon as I had learned what is reported in the previous paragraph and without having learned who are the occupants of the castle or what takes place when they meet together, assuming that they do so meet, then I resembled Henry James in my not wanting to learn more than a few ingredients, so to call them, but unlike James I was not yet aware that I had acquired my ingredients. My only reaction at the time was to admire the Swede for what I took to be a considerable achievement and to read no further about him and his film lest

I learn that my admiration was misplaced. His achievement, so I supposed, was his having discovered, late in life, that a true work of art in no way depends for its justification on its seeming connections with the place that many call the real world and I call the visible world.

I would have watched several of the Swede's films during the 1960s, which was the last decade when I still hoped to learn from films. After I had written the previous sentence, I set about recalling whatever images I could recall from those films. I recalled first an image of a white-haired man looking out over a small lake; behind the man is a house of two or, perhaps, three storeys. I then recalled a certain expression on the face of a ragged boy of ten or twelve years. The boy and his two ragged men-companions had completed, moments before, the rape and murder of a young woman, hardly more than a girl, after they had met up with her in a clearing in a forest. Moments after I had seen the face of the ragged boy, he vomited.

I was about to ask the questions why am I able to call to mind only those two images from the many thousands of images that would have appeared to me while I watched the Swede's films during the 1960s? Do those images have for me any seeming connection with the place that I call the visible world? And, if the images seem to have no such connection, what connection, if any, do they have with the place that I call the invisible world or, sometimes for convenience, my mind? First, however, I had better reassure the discerning reader that I am well aware of the many falsehoods in the previous paragraph – falsehoods that

I allowed into the text for the sake of the undiscerning reader, who might have found tedious a strictly accurate account of what is reported there. I reported, accurately enough, that I had recalled an *image* of a white-haired man but thereafter I fell into everyday language, so to call it, such as probably caused many an undiscerning reader to see in mind images of an actual-seeming ragged boy and actual-seeming ragged men and to forget that what were, in fact, denoted were mental images, or memories, as some would call them, of images projected through film onto a screen fifty years before their recall. At the risk of trying the patience of the discerning reader, I shall add that much else denoted by my everyday language in the previous paragraph has no existence in the world where I sit writing these words. The image of a man looking out over a lake with a tall house behind him was an image of an image of a man pretending so to look. No young woman, hardly more than a girl, was raped and murdered. No ragged boy actually vomited. Even so, I have kept in mind for fifty years images of these nullities. As for the questions that I was about to ask when I began to write this paragraph, I can best answer them figuratively. If ever I should choose to locate those images and many others of their kind at one particular site, as the Swede, late in life, chose to locate the chief characters of his many films, then the site would be at the centre of some mental landscape of mostly level grassy countryside and would comprise a house of two or, perhaps, three storeys and who knows how many windows.

I would not brand as undiscerning any reader of the previous paragraph who might look forward to reading in this present paragraph what he or she would probably call a description of the house mentioned above. I would expect, however, that any such reader, after a little reflection, would agree that what he or she wanted from me was that I should report not the appearance of a particular house but the detail that first alerted me to the existence of the house in what I call the invisible world, which detail would surely have seemed likely to fufill some or another long-held hope or expectation of mine. I would expect also that any such reader, after having read my report, would see in mind just such a house as he or she had for long hoped or expected to see while reading some or another passage of fiction.

In the year when I became married, in the mid-1960s, I read the first volume of the autobiography of a male writer who was almost thirty years older than I and who had died fifteen years later after having been struck by a car when walking drunkenly across the street in a provincial city of this state. I remember my observing while I read his autobiography that the author used the present tense throughout the book and my deciding soon afterwards that I ought myself to use that tense throughout the work of fiction that I had been trying for several years to write. After having begun to write this paragraph, I remembered several details from my experience as a reader, nearly fifty years ago, of the autobiography mentioned, but the only one of those details that I was able to remember *before* I began to write the paragraph was my seeming to see dazzling points of light on a distant hillside during moments while I read that the author claimed to remember his having seen often as a child, while he watched from a balcony in the late afternoon, and when the light from the declining sun fell at a certain angle, what he called sumless distant windows like spots of golden oil.

Given that the book in my hands was an autobiography, I surely supposed, when I first read the report of the glowing widows, that the author himself had seen several times during his childhood just such windows as he claimed to have seen. Today, having read and written much during nearly fifty years since, I suppose no such thing. Today, I understand that so-called autobiography is only one of the least worthy varieties of fiction extant. Given that what I read was in the present tense, and recalling now how young I was at the time and how little I had read, I can hardly doubt that I supposed also, when I first read the report of the glowing windows, that what I was then experiencing as a reader was the nearest equivalent that I could hope to experience to whatever it was that the author would have experienced, nearly thirty years before my birth, when he sometimes saw from a balcony in the late afternoon reflected sunlight in distant windows. Today, having read and written and supposed much during nearly fifty years since, I suppose no such thing.

While I was reading the report of the richly lit distant windows, I would probably have counted myself fortunate to know the approximate location, in the world where I then sat reading, of the actual balcony where the author of the autobiography was reported to have watched often as a child and of the distant hillside where the windows were strangely lit. Earlier in the text, the author had named the street where he had lived during certain years of his childhood. I happened to know that same street and was even able to visualise, while I read, an approximation of the distant hillside where the windows had sometimes reflected the late sunlight. I suspect that I would have paused soon after I had read the passage in which the windows were compared to drops of golden oil and would have speculated as follows. Given that I know the very street where the autobiographer lived during certain years of his childhood, and given further that I am able to visualise, while I read, an approximation of the actual hillside that he sometimes saw in the distance, I am more fortunate than the many readers who do not know the street and are unable to visualise the hillside. I am more fortunate because I am able, if I choose, to visit nowadays the very street from which the autobiographer looked out sometimes at least twenty years before my birth, to wait in the street until a certain moment on a certain sort of late afternoon, and then to assess the aptness of the autobiographer's comparing a number of distant windows to sumless spots of golden oil. Today, having read and written and speculated much during nearly fifty years since, I could never thus speculate.

Once, or it may have been more than once, during the mid-1940s, I travelled with my parents and my siblings by road from a large provincial city in the north of this state to a smaller city in the south-west. We stopped for our midday meal in a large city in the inner west of the state – the same city, as it happens,

where the autobiographer, more than thirty years later, would
be struck and killed while drunkenly crossing a street. Travel
by road was far slower then than now, and we spent most of
the afternoon travelling further towards the smaller city, our
destination. When the sun was low in the sky, we were still
crossing the extensive plains that occupy much of the south-west
of this state. If this paragraph were part of an autobiography
or of a conventional work of fiction, then I might well report at
this point that I saw at least once, and far across the extensive
plains mentioned, a sight that I surmised was a reflection of the
light from the declining sun in one or more upper windows of a
house of at least two storeys. I might even go on to report that my
reading, twenty years later, a certain autobiographical passage
in which distant windows are likened to spots of golden oil was
in some way connected with my reporting, in the next-to-last
paragraph of my first published work of fiction, that the chief
character of that work, while travelling with his parents across
the extensive plains mentioned, is enabled to see in mind certain
details that he has previously been unable so to see. This present
work being neither autobiography nor fiction of the same order
as the work that I began to write, in the present tense, in the
mid-1960s, I need report here only the detail first mentioned in
the seventh paragraph of this present work. I need report here
only that the window first mentioned in the first paragraph of
this present work of fiction might have seemed, at the moment
when it was first mentioned, as a distant window might have
seemed on an extensive plain to a narrator of an autobiography

or to a chief character of a work of fiction – might have seemed like a spot of golden oil, even though I myself have never seen any window with such an appearance.

One of the many devices employed by writers of fiction is the use of the present tense. I myself have written several works of fiction in the present tense. Soon after I had read the autobiography in which distant windows are likened to spots of golden oil, I began yet another of the drafts that I had already begun of a work of fiction that I had for long had in mind. The draft then begun was in the present tense, and when I had completed the draft, five years later, it remained so. Had I simply imitated the technique, so to call it, of the autobiographer? Had I supposed that my using the present tense would cause my reader sometimes to pause, as I had once paused after having read that certain distant windows resembled spots of golden oil? Had I further supposed that my having paused at that moment was the result of my having observed that the windows mentioned in the text seemed at that moment as clearly visible and their effect on me as palpable as if I had been observing actual windows from an actual distance? If I had thus supposed, then I might well have believed that the reading of a work of fiction resembles the watching of a film and even that the text of a work of fiction ought to resemble a film-script. I prefer to suppose that my using the present tense was in some way connected with my having reported in the first paragraph of my first work of fiction that the chief character, a boy of nine years, is looking at a page of a calendar published by a religious order of the Catholic church in which calendar each of the twelve pages has in its lower half a grid of black lines on a background of yellow. For the chief character, the black and the yellow represent not a sequence of days but a map of remembered experiences in the provincial city where he lives; the black suggests the narrow strips of bitumen on the streets in the suburbs of the city while the yellow suggests the broad margins of those streets and the mostly unpaved footpaths, all of which are strewn with bright gravel from the former goldfields of the district. And just as he is able to follow any number of routes through the black and the yellow, so the boy, when he remembers, takes no account of any fixed temporal boundaries or sequences. As for the upper half of each page of the calendar, which is occupied by a coloured reproduction of some or another painting of Biblical scenes or characters, the boy has learned from his parents and his teachers that his and their world is overhung by an altogether superior world, and if he has not learned also that that world has no days and no nights then he could hardly have failed to suppose that a personage looking thence down at his, the boy's, world would see not a record of something called time but a richly detailed map of an immense landscape.

For reasons that are no part of this work of fiction, I was required, thirty and more years ago, to read several books purporting to instruct readers in the techniques of fiction-writing. The books were divided into chapters with headings such as *Plot*,

Characters, *Dialogue*, and *Theme and Meaning*. I long ago forgot most of what I read in the books, but while I was writing the previous paragraph I recalled something of what I read in a certain chapter headed *Flashbacks and Time Shifts*. I recalled not actual words but rather their import. I recalled the author's advising the intending writer of fiction to prepare the reader before introducing into the narrative any so-called flashback or time-shift. Thus, the writer might have a character look out from a car or a train at an apple-orchard before introducing as a flashback a scene from the character's childhood, which scene would have for its setting a garden overhung by an apple-tree. I can hardly believe that anything so foolish was once delivered as advice to intending writers. The author of the advice was himself a writer of fiction, although I forget his name and the titles of his two or three books, and I supposed, even when I first read his advice on flashbacks and time-shifts, that he had in mind, while he wrote, those films in which the pages of a desk-calendar fly back rapidly or in which the face of a staring or a sleeping character is obscured by swirling mists as a signal to the viewer that what follows is a scene from the past.

I am not about to assert, as the narrator asserted in a piece of fiction of mine first published twenty-five years ago, that time is non-existent and that what we denote by the word *time* is no more than our moving from one to another place in an infinite expanse. Instead, I restrict myself to claiming only that no sort of time exists in a work of fiction such as this, the setting of which is place after place in what I called earlier the invisible world.

The reader might care to observe how easily he or she reads the following paragraph, even though the matters there reported have no temporal connection with the matters reported in this and the previous few paragraphs.

Soon after I had read, in a weekly news-magazine from perhaps twenty-five years ago, a reference to a certain castle or, rather, to a certain image-castle, I began, as I ought to have reported earlier, to write this work of fiction. And yet I was still, it seemed, not wholly free from the influence of films that I had watched long before and could hardly recall. I foresaw myself writing, for example, about a man who preferred not to draw the blind or the curtain of his room except on a certain few afternoons of the year. If I had gone ahead with my first, misguided scheme, this, the fifth section of the book, would have comprised a brief account of a man who never failed, during every year of his long life, to mark certain days in late spring or in early summer. Those had been the days during his childhood when he had felt urged to draw the blind in the single window of the loungeroom of his parents' house in a provincial city in the north of this state and then to raise the window slightly so that the north wind would agitate the worn brown blind and would cause to appear in the dim room flashes of the fierce light from outside. Influenced, surely, by scenes from a film I had never seen nor would ever see – a film set in a castle known to me only from a single sentence in an article in a news-magazine – I foresaw myself writing first about a man who would enact, as though for the benefit of a watcher, some or another ritual from his childhood as a demonstration that his life was all of a piece. Perhaps I even envisaged him in his dim room, on a day of hot north winds, as handling again some of the collection of glass marbles that he had kept by him throughout his life – the same marbles that had represented racehorses in one of his childhood rituals. But this misguided scheme, as I called it, not only seemed more suited to film than to fiction but lacked an appropriate setting. And then I, who have never seen any sort of castle nor any sort of European scenery, saw in mind an image of the only building where my true subject-matter might come into being and, around the building, the only scenery likely to surround such a building; and I foresaw myself writing not about pretend-characters enacting pretend-rituals but about fictional personages writing, on day after day during year after year, in a building of two or, perhaps, three storeys having several wings and numerous windows and being surrounded by mostly level grassy countryside.

The discerning reader, whether or not he or she allows my claim that no sort of time exists in a work of fiction such as this, might well consider me inconsistent or even confused to have used the past tense of most of the verbs in this work. If these paragraphs report events, so to call them, in a timeless location or an eternal present, why am I not obliged to use verbs in the present tense?

If my mood were wilful, I might reply that my way of writing is intended to prevent even an undiscerning reader from trying to apprehend my subject-matter in the way that a viewer, or so I suppose, apprehends the subject-matter of a film. A more respectful reply might include the information that these paragraphs are examples of what I call *considered narration* and the claim that the reader of such paragraphs is entitled to suppose hardly more than that the narrator of the paragraphs was alive at the time when they were written and felt urged to report certain matters.

The reader's entitlements are limited indeed, but of course he or she, while reading a considered narrative, postulates or supposes with little regard for any such limits. Many a reader, for example, might seem while reading to hear what might be called the voice behind the narrative or even to see what might be called the personage behind it. The narrator, of course, knows nothing of such matters but I, the narrator of this work of fiction, am hopeful that many a discerning reader has understood by now why a piece of considered narration ought to include verbs in both the present and the past tense; has understood that a considered narrative reports both that certain events may have taken place, or may have seemed to take place, and also what it is to have knowledge of these matters.

The previous sentence seemed, while I was composing it, a most apt ending for this, the sixth section of this work of fiction. However, I found just now, among the scribbled pages meant to prompt me while I composed the section, certain notes that

I could not bring myself to leave unused. One note was intended to remind me of something that I heard from a university lecturer in Islamic philosophy nearly fifty years ago, when I was a mature-age student in a faculty of arts. What may have been the lecturer's purpose in telling his class what he told them I long ago forgot, if ever I understood it, although it was surely to do with the phenomenon that we call *time*. He asked us to call to mind a motor-car travelling on a road across a mostly level landscape. A person standing close beside the road and looking directly ahead would be aware for some time that the car has not yet reached him or her, then, for a brief time, that the car is present to his or her sight and then, for some time afterwards, that the car is no longer present, even if still audible. The lecturer then asked us to call to mind a person looking towards the road from an upper window of a building at some distance away. This person is aware of the car as being present to his or her sight during the whole time while it seems to be approaching, present to the sight of, and then travelling away from the person beside the road.

While I was writing the previous paragraph, it occurred to me that the lecturer mentioned might have been trying to explain the notion of eternity and that the observer in the upper room, for whom the present is prolonged, as it were, is meant to call to mind none other than God, who from a vantage-point beyond the last of the stars sees all human history as eternally present. Commentators on works of fiction sometimes have used terms such as *god-like* to describe the extensive knowledge that certain narrators lay claim to: knowledge of the thoughts and feelings of more than one character in the one fictional work and also a view, so to call it, ranging over many fictional settings and over the fictional present and past. I myself have never laid claim to any such knowledge, but sometimes while writing this and the previous paragraph I felt as though mine might not be the only view of my subject-matter. I felt as an observer might feel when he or she strains to look across some or another mostly level landscape while behind him or her some or another personage sees from an upper window all that the observer strains to see and more.

It would be absurd to suppose that the experience of some or another personage looking out from an upper window of a building of two or, perhaps, three storeys must be different in quality from that of some or another personage strolling in the grounds below. Nor do I intend to make the familiar claim that the personages reported as living fictional lives in this or any other work of fiction are somehow outside or beyond what we know as time; that such personages exist in some sort of timeless realm often assumed to be superior to our own. (Surely a person is able to sample the experience of eternity without having to read fiction? I found just now a passage that I copied more than thirty years ago from the translated writings of Alfred Jarry: 'It is fine to live two different moments of time as one: that alone allows one authentically to live a single moment of eternity, indeed all eternity since it has no moments.') What I was hoping to do when I began this paragraph was to explain, for myself as much as for the reader, why I cannot call to mind any detail of a certain house of two or, perhaps, three storeys (the silent corridors in the far-reaching wings, for example, or the grounds where strollers readily lose their way among hedges or thickets or ferneries, or the immense and mostly level distances to be seen from upper windows) without the conviction that the personages frequenting the place exist not in any sort of temporal progression but in what might be called the *narrative dimension*, which not only extends infinitely backwards and forwards, as we might say of our own *time*, as we call it, but has what I perceive to be a breadth or depth, likewise immeasurable.

How should I begin this paragraph? A certain male personage often recalls that he spent much time as a child looking at reproductions of famous paintings and wondering about a matter that he supposed would be for ever beyond his power to resolve. I was wrong to use the word *wondering* in the previous sentence. Surely no one, in fact, wonders. Surely we postulate, speculate, or supply possible answers rather than remain agape and vacant-minded. What I ought to have written was that the personage spent much time as a child seeing in mind whatever was out of his sight in the backgrounds of famous paintings, or to either side of the places depicted there, or in the sight of those painted personages who looked not towards their painter or their viewer but at persons, places, or things forever invisible to both. Given that the personage mentioned saw as a child no other reproductions of paintings apart from the twelve on the upper halves of the pages of a certain calendar sent each year as a Christmas gift to his parents by a certain devout sister of his father, most of the depicted personages that he saw were divinities or angels or saints or Biblical characters, and most of the narratives that they were caught up in were already known to him. He was therefore obliged at an early age to discover some more promising task than the envisaging of sights intended merely to inspire devotion or to promote piety in the viewer. Instead of following the gaze of kneeling worshippers upwards and past the seated Madonna and Infant or the all-seeing, all-comprehending stare of the God-man into heaven itself, he learned soon enough to see or, rather, to envisage for himself. He would send into the hilly and forested or the level and grassy backgrounds of certain paintings a version of himself hopeful of finding, beyond the last blurs and tints, a folk who were moved more by the vague or the imprecise or the random than by the certainties of religion; a folk for whom a complicated game of chance or a half-heard melody or an inexplicable dream commanded more attention than a prayer or a holy text. Or he might remain deliberately alone in the hope of meeting up with another of his own rare kind: someone, preferably female, who had found her way past the last hint of a horizon on a coloured page that he had never seen nor would ever see.

As soon as he had been able to make sense of books, he had learned that he was far more free to stray in his reading than in his observing of painted scenes. He had struggled to insert himself, as it were, into many a setting that hung before his eyes, but while he read he was hardly aware of having crossed any fixed boundary. And yet his being at home among denoted settings and personages was only the beginning of his pleasure. When he paused from following the text, or even when one or another book was far from his reach, even then he had access not only to narrated scenes and events but also to a far more extensive fictional space, so to call it.

He found it impossible to accept that the last page of a book of fiction was any sort of boundary or limit. For him, the personages who had first appeared while he was reading some or another fictional text were no less alive after the text itself had come to an end than while he had pored over it. This is surely a common experience, but he wanted more than to brood over only those scenes and events that the narrators of works of fiction had allowed him to read about. What he did as a child was hardly more than to daydream about the unrecorded future lives of personages reported to be still alive when last written about, although he sometimes tried to write a few pages of his own to report what he hoped might happen to them or had already happened to them in some or another time-scheme beyond his comprehension. In the years when he would have been called an adolescent, certain personages who owed their existence to his having read certain details into certain works of fiction seemed not only closer to him than any of his family or his friends but closer even than the divine or sanctified personages that he believed to be watching his every deed and thought. Not only did the fictional personages, so to call them, seem closer than the religious, so to call them, but whereas the religious seemed ready always to judge him or to censure him, the fictional world seemed to want no more from him than that he should side with them rather than with the religious, even though his doing so would earn him not eternal salvation but the right to live with them, the fictional ones, for perhaps no more than a few days of their peculiar, immeasurable version of time.

Until as late as his twentieth year, he dared not consider the eternity promoted by his pastors and his teachers as less than factual or the mysterious time-scale of the fiction he read as anything more than a beguiling illusion. One of his heroes during his first twenty years was an uncle of his, an unmarried brother of his father and a brother also of the devout unmarried woman who was the sender each year of the calendars mentioned earlier. This man, who was hardly less devout than the sender of the calendars, several times during the first twenty years of the chief character of these fictional pages deplored in his hearing the number of young men who lost their faith and gave up the practice of their religion as a result of their dealings with some or another, or with more than one, young woman. During an exchange of letters in a year soon after the chief character had lost his faith and had given up the practice of his religion and had preferred not to meet with his devout uncle and aunt, the uncle had put it to the nephew that the true cause of his lapsing, as he, the uncle, called it, had been some or another, or more than one, young woman. The chief character had denied his uncle's claim, but he, the chief character, had acknowledged to himself that the claim was accurate, although not in the sense that his uncle would have intended. He, the chief character, far from lusting after and then taking up with or cohabiting with some or another, or more than one, young woman, (the sentences hereabouts report fictional events purporting to have taken place during the fictional 1950s) had decided – no, had accepted what had seemed from the moment of his acceptance to have been inevitable since the time when he had first read the first page of fiction that had made sense to him (the chief character would have been some or another fictional female) and from the time when he had written the first sentence of fiction that he could later recall (the subject was some or another fictional young female). He had accepted, at some or another moment while he was reading some or another poem by A.E. Housman or some or another work of fiction by Thomas Hardy, that his most urgent need was not to perfect himself so that his soul would later be admitted to a heaven without end but to bring into being some or another fictional version of himself that would be able to move unchallenged, if only during a few fictional hours or days, among the unfulfilled lads of Shropshire; nor to burn with the devotion to some or another deity or virgin-mother of sanctified personage, but to convey by some or another means to some or another female personage in some or another work of fiction by Thomas Hardy that a fictional version of himself was in sympathy with her.

The previous four paragraphs may be thought of as having been written behind some or another upper window in a house of two or, perhaps, three storeys and in some or another room opening off a corridor frequented by, among others, those wayward few who look for their subject-matter not in visible places on the far side of the mostly level grassy countryside surrounding this building but in the mental space surrounding fictional texts, which space is to be thought of as reaching endlessly backwards, so to speak, from the first paragraph of each text, endlessly forward, so to speak, from the final paragraph, and endlessly sideways, so to speak, from every intervening paragraph. The wayward few, as I call them, take for their subject-matter scenes and events never reported in any fictional text but likely to have taken place in the vast zone of possibility surrounding not just every page but the merest sentence on that page. And the mental space that I mentioned just now extends so far in every direction from every fictional text that the wayward ones, as I call them, are able to write as though the content of many a seemingly separate fictional text adjoins, or is entangled with, the content of many another such.

One of the terms often appearing in books meant to instruct intending writers of fiction is *point-of-view*. Being an unscholarly person, I can only speculate as to when some or another writer of fiction or commentator on fiction first devised the term, which he or she surely did in an effort to describe and, partly, to explain a process that countless readers of fiction and nearly as many writers of it had engaged in for centuries past and engage in to this day without troubling themselves to examine it. The result of the process is that the reader (myself and, surely, not a few others excluded) is persuaded that he or she stands in relation to one or more fictional personages as no one in the world where I sit writing these words could ever stand in relation to another: the reader (excluding those noted earlier in this sentence) is persuaded that he or she knows what the fictional personage thinks, feels, remembers, hopes for, fears, and much else. I am not concerned here with the manifest folly of the reader thus persuaded: the reader who wants from fiction an experience hardly more subtle than the viewer gets from a film. I prefer to suppose that the discerning reader of *this* work of fiction needs no further reminder from me in the matter. Perhaps even the discerning reader, however, is unaware of the many variations of the process that goes nowadays by the name *point-of-view*. At one extreme is the boldness and directness of the nineteenth-century writer of fiction who informs the reader, as though possessing an unchallenged right to do so, that this or that character is contented or disconnected or weighed down with remorse or uplifted by hope. Many a writer of this sort ranges freely from character to character, even within the same few pages, with the result that the reader might be enabled to know the intentions of each of two characters in a dispute between antagonists, for example, or a proposal of marriage. One such passage that occurs to me reports the scene, so to call it, in *Tess of the d'Urbervilles*, by Thomas Hardy, in which Tess Durbeyfield and Alec d'Urberville meet for the first time. The narrator reports in the same few pages not only Tess's thoughts and feelings but some of what occurs to Alec when he first meets her and even the motives of Alec's dead father, he who had built the mansion in front of which Tess and Alec meet and had appropriated the ancient surname that seemingly linked the two characters. I quote here a short paragraph from the chapter titled 'The Maiden'.

Tess's sense of a certain ludicrousness in her errand was now so strong that, notwithstanding her awe of him, and her general discomfort at being here, her rosy lips curved towards a smile, much to the attraction of the swarthy Alexander.

I quoted the lines above for no other purpose than to show how a certain sort of author of fiction claims to know the thoughts and feelings of more than one of his or her characters and will sometimes report in a single sentence, as the narrator reports in the quoted passage, the viewpoints, so to call them, of two, but while I was copying the sentence above, I noticed, for the first time that I could recall, the seeming incongruity of the adverb *here*. I then read the paragraphs before and after the paragraph that includes the quoted sentence. In those paragraphs, the author moves freely, as it were, among his characters, so to call them. At some or another moment, he might seem to lean closely towards one or another character while he reports, in the person of the narrator, the thoughts and feelings of that character. Soon afterwards, according to the time-scale of the narrative, the author might seem privy to the thoughts and feelings of quite a different character. Soon afterwards again, the same author might seem to step noticeably backwards from all of the characters and, far from seeming to loiter furtively, with bowed head and downcast eyes, in range of the sighs and murmurings of this or that character, might seem to fling back his head and to look far outwards and upwards while he reports to the reader not only the broad outlines of the far-reaching fictional landscapes surrounding the cramped cottage-garden or the tiny parlour where he had learned, not long before, the secrets of those characters, but the fold upon fold of field and forest surrounding garden and parlour and even the sight of distant villages and towns that he, the far-seeing author, but none of his characters might have been aware of and, this being the boldest of all his authorial claims, the history of all that he claimed to see or, should I say, the tendencies that he divined in the history, its moral purpose or the lack thereof, and the pressure of that history on his characters, whether or not they perceived it.

The sort of author who practises this narratory nimbleness might seem sometimes, even to the discerning reader and, more importantly, even to himself or herself, the nimble narrator, to be present in the place that he or she happens to be writing about rather than in the place where he or she sits writing. If I, a reader of average discernment, saw, while I read the passage quoted above, a translucent image of an elderly man derived from a few reproductions of photographs in some or another biography – saw the ghostly image sometimes lurking near this or that character, then perhaps the author of the passage would have seemed sometimes, while he was writing the same passage or similar passages, to be present in the setting, so to call it, of his own fiction. And yet, despite such brief impressions, he, the author, could surely never have supposed, while he composed his actual sentences, that he was doing so anywhere else but in the visible world while his characters, so to call them, were elsewhere.

Why, then, did not Thomas Hardy, when reporting indirectly the reaction of his character Tess to her being in a certain fictional place and in the presence of his character Alexander – why did not Hardy use the adverb *there* but its opposite *here*? An actor in a film would use the word *here* when referring to her situation. Likewise, a character in a work of fiction by an author with no more worthy aim than to have his or her characters seem to be actors in a film – such a character would report himself or herself to be *here*. But Thomas Hardy was using the traditional form of wholly indirect fictional narration in which all fictional events are presumed to have taken place during a fictional past and at a fictional distance, as it were, from the places where authors write and readers read and was therefore obliged by convention to write not *here* but *there*. Other readers of Thomas Hardy may conclude far otherwise, but I choose to conclude that he, Hardy, on at least one occasion during the countless hours while he wrote fiction or while he had in mind fictional subject-matter, seemed to be in the presence of one or more of his characters, so to call them. He may have supposed himself to be standing on the same soil where stood Tess Durbeyfield and Alec d'Urberville, or he may have supposed those two to be standing beside his desk; whatever he supposed, I derive much encouragement from the mere fact of his having supposed it and I believe that he would have supposed similarly on other occasions, even if his grammar offers no evidence for this. I derive much encouragement, I who have been always a timid author, but the residents of a certain upper storey in a certain wing of a building of two or, perhaps, three storeys may for long have considered self-evident my hesitant conclusions and all that follows from them.

At the other extreme from Thomas Hardy and his like are those writers of fiction who became increasingly numerous during the twentieth century and whose narratives report the thoughts and motives and such of only the chief character. This character is often of the same gender as is the author, and some at least of his or her fictional experiences can be seen to resemble the actual experiences of the author. However far-reaching or however narrow might be the view, so to call it, of the narrator, whenever I read a fictional text I am never unaware of his or her fictional presence. What happens in my mind hours or days or years after I have read such a text may be far otherwise, but for as long as the text is in front of my eyes I am mindful of its being a fictional text: sentence after sentence composed by a human agent. I seem to hear the written words as being transmitted to me in a sort of silent speech, however absurd that expression might seem. I cannot hear, or seem to hear, such speech without seeing, or seeming to see, the personage responsible for it, and even though my reporting what follows may be evidence of credulousness or gullibility on my part, I confess that my first impulse is usually to trust the narrator; to regard him or her as reliable. At this point, the discerning reader wants to know how

I react in the presence of a narrator whom I suspect of being unreliable or when confronted by one of those curious texts sometimes published as fiction but having the appearance of diary-entries or collections of letters or other documents. I have no answer for the discerning reader, but I can state for his or her benefit that I decline to read any piece of fiction if I suspect the author of believing that fiction is mere artifice and that the reader of fiction has no more urgent need than to be diverted or teased. (Even the undiscerning reader should have learned from the previous sentence that the narrator of this present work of fiction is to be trusted.)

I have mentioned so far only third-person narrators and none of my sort of narrator, who writes in the first person. The undiscerning reader may be surprised to learn that first-person narrators are hardly less varied than third-person narrators if they are classified according to how much or how little they claim to know. In fact, almost all first-person narrators during the past century have been of the one sort: reporters of their own thoughts and feelings and also of what they observe of the doings of other fictional participants. At the other extreme from these limited narrators, as they might be called, are those – mostly from the nineteenth century and earlier – who seem to report for the most part in the conventional mode of far-seeing and knowledgeable third-person narrator but who report occasionally in the first person. Anthony Trollope, in some at least of his novels, narrates thus. I seem to recall a few examples of such narration in the novels of Thomas Hardy. At a further remove even from these

writers and their kind is Henry James, who will be mentioned
later in this work of fiction, he being of much interest to some
of the occupants of an upper floor of a certain building of two
or, perhaps, three storeys. Whereas my instinct is to trust a
third-person narrator, I am wary of several kinds of first-person
narrator. I cannot bring myself to read any fictional text issuing
from a pretend-narrator, as I call any purported first-person
narrator of a different gender from the author of the text or from
a different historical world. I could not read, for example, a first-
person narrative by a female personage if the author is known to
be male. Nor could I read a first-person narrative by a personage
who is obviously derived from a grandparent or a forebear of the
author. The sort of first-person narrative that most repels me has
for its purported narrator a personage who could never have
had the wit to recite the narrative, let alone the verbal skills to set
it down in writing. The late-twentieth-century American writer
Raymond Carver wrote many stories purporting to be narrated
by pretend-narrators, as I call them. I object to such fiction
because it claims to be other than fiction; because it makes the
same absurd claim that a film makes: the claim that its subject-
matter is of the same order as what is commonly called *real* or
true or *actual*. Fiction, even what I call true fiction, is fiction.
An author demeans fiction if he or she requires the reader to
believe that what happens in his or her mind while reading is no
different from what happens over his or her shoulder or outside
his or her window. What happens in the mind of the reader of
true fiction is richer and more memorable by far than anything

seen through the lens of a camera or overheard by an author in a bar or a trailer park.

Even the discerning reader who is also a student of narration – even he or she might struggle so far to classify the narrator of this present work and might struggle further as the work becomes more complicated in later pages. It is not for me to define myself, as it were. The reader should think of me as a *personage* as being in some respects less than an actual person and in other respects rather more so. At the very least, I am a voice: the voice behind the text. At the risk of confusing the undiscerning reader, I might well describe myself as the voice of another sort of personage who has been scarcely mentioned as yet in this work: the author or, rather, the *implied* author, by which I mean the personage of whom nothing is known except what can be inferred from this text. At the very least, I am a voice, but who knows what I might not seem to the discerning and sympathetic reader before he or she has read to the end of these pages, which are, let it be remembered, a sequence of sentences composed by a human hand long before they sounded to any reader as though recited by a mere voice.

I mentioned earlier in this section my being impelled to trust fictional narrators. This must not be taken to mean that I consider the subject-matter of a trustworthy narrator as anything but fiction. Never, while reading any novel by Thomas Hardy, for example, would I mistake, or even wish to be able to mistake, the text in front of me for a report of actual matters or a description of actual persons in actual places. I acknowledge that many another reader looks to fiction for what he or she might call a deeper understanding of actual persons or events or moral issues, so to call them. I am well aware that scholars are able to name actual or historical persons or places that are the originals, so to speak, or the inspiration for fictional counterparts. (Only the other day, I found in a handsome illustrated selection of poems by Thomas Hardy a reproduction of a painting with the title 'Tess's Cottage and Evershot Church'. I have already forgotten most of the details of the reproduction. Nor am I curious to learn why the cottage is so named. If it is claimed to have some or another connection with the fictional character Tess Durbeyfield, then I can only marvel at how far the depicted cottage is from any of the scenery where I have located the fictional personage known to me as Tess Durbeyfield during the past fifty and more years.) Even so, I can only state what clear-sighted observation has taught me, which is that many a fictional character, so to call him or her, has become, from the moment when I first learned of his or her fictional existence, a far from fictional personage in a far from fictional setting that happens to be, among other things, the setting for this and every other of my works of fiction. And if I report that I trust certain narrators, I am thereby announcing my confidence that those fictional presences would approve of the previous sentence.

———————

One of the many sorts of fiction that became briefly fashionable during the past fifty years was called by most commentators *self-referential fiction.* I can recall reading several examples of such fiction in the 1970s, or was it the 1980s? Self-referential fiction was never more than a small part of the body of fiction published at the time, but those who wrote it or praised it seemed to suppose that no sort of self-referential works of fiction had been published in earlier times and, predictably, that writers and readers would soon agree that self-referential fiction was better able than more traditional modes to achieve the aims of fiction, whatever they might be. In the 1970s and the 1980s, I was easily deceived as a reader. Even so, I was just sufficiently alert to be able privately to refute the claims of the advocates of self-referential fiction. I had read *Tristram Shandy* and some of the fiction of Anthony Trollope and much of the fiction of Thomas Hardy. I admit that I was dazzled at first by *If on a Winter's Night a Traveller*, by Italo Calvino, but I did not fail to note soon afterwards how little I could recall of its intricate contrivances or of the seeming-qualities of its glib narrator, not to mention its stock characters, and if I think of the book nowadays I think of its author as someone for whom writer and reader are opposed to one another as the players on either side of a chessboard are opposed. Even the undiscerning reader of this fiction of mine should have understood by now that I, the narrator, would dread to feel that we were separated even by these sentences.

I can recall today no instance of my admiring some or another work of self-referential fiction, much less of my trying to write such a work. (I will explain briefly in the following paragraph why this present work of fiction is not self-referential, although it may have seemed so already to a certain sort of undiscerning reader.) The more extreme examples of their kind repelled me. The narrators of these works would sometimes pause in their reporting and would affect to be unable to decide which of several possible courses of events should follow from that point or, as an undiscerning reader might say, what should happen to the chief characters. And yet, I myself was not discerning enough at that time to be able to explain to myself why I turned away instinctively from such writing.

The narrators who postured in front of their readers and who wondered aloud, as it were, what fates to assign to various characters, were deriving enjoyment, so I now believe, from what they supposed was the dispelling of an illusion held by most, if not all, of their readers. The illusion is that the characters described in fiction are, if not actual persons of the same order as the readers themselves, ideal persons, so to call them, who live out their lives in the same sorts of place as are depicted in films while their authors are required merely to report on them in the way that the makers of films observe *their* characters. It is not for me to guess how many readers of fiction might be under the illusion mentioned or how many of the deluded, so to call them, might have revised their beliefs after having read that the subject-matter of fiction depended on the mere whim of some or another belittler of the long-held trust between reader and narrator. All that I can do is to state here what seems to me self-evident: while the writer and the reader, together with the words that they write or read, may be seen to exist in this, the visible world, what they are pleased or driven to write about or to read about – their subject-matter – is nowhere to be seen: those seeming persons and seeming events and the seeming scenery behind them are present to one writer alone or one reader alone in the cramped foreground of somewhere vast and vague; and while I would never presume to understand the laws or principles operating in either of the two places – the visible or the invisible – I could never doubt that those in the one differ greatly from those in the other and could never consider any writer claiming otherwise to be anything but a fool.

I recalled just now an earlier undertaking of mine to explain in the previous paragraph why this is not a self-referential work of fiction. The discerning reader should have found the promised explanation in the paragraph as it stands. For the sake of the undiscerning reader, I shall repeat the simple fact that I am the narrator of this work and not the author. In the matter of my fate, so to call it, I am no more able to exercise choice than is any narrator of any of the texts going forward in room after room in this wing of the house of two or, perhaps, three storeys where this text is to be understood as going forward, or any character, so to call him or her, in any work of fiction reported to be going forward in any of those rooms.

The subject-matter of a work of true fiction may be understood as extending infinitely backwards and forwards, for want of better terms to denote the twin axes of what I called earlier the narrative dimension. The same subject-matter may also be understood as extending infinitely sideways in opposite directions, and again I use words less than appropriate for concepts seldom written about. Had I been more mindful of this when I began the fifth section of this work, then I might well have written such as the following.

He had been attracted, during his long lifetime, by hundreds, perhaps thousands of female faces. He had no doubt that if ever he were to visit one or another parlour or reception room where visitors were received in the distant wing that was said to be occupied mostly by females – he had no doubt that he would see there during his first visit one at least of the sort of female whose face would cause him to suppose, before he knew her name or the least detail about her, that she might be better disposed towards him and less bothered by his peculiar ways than many another of her gender and age-group. He had long ago given up trying to define, or even to isolate, the features of the faces that drew him. He recognised, however, that the hair framing the face was more likely to be dark than otherwise. This, then, was all that he knew about her whom he was likely to see in the distant wing, wherever it might have been: that her hair was dark. And although he had not the least intention of visiting the place, he was readily able to foresee what would happen if he did so: his looking at her for what he believed was no longer than some or another man might have looked at some or another woman who held no interest for him but his learning soon afterwards from her way of looking at him that he had given himself away yet again, by looking either more often or more intently than he had been aware, and that she had learned about him already what he hoped she might not learn until much later, if at all.

He had never been able to make sense of the theories popular during his time for their seeming to explain the workings of the mind. In this, as in every other field that interested him, he trusted in his concern for particulars and for details. What others might have called *meaning* he called *connectedness*, and he trusted that he would one day see (revelation being for him always a visual matter) among the multitudes of details that he thought of as his life or as his experience faint lines seeming to link what he had never previously thought of as being linked and the emergence of a rudimentary pattern, which word had always been one of his favourites.

He had forgotten, of course, many of the dark-haired females. He recalled most clearly those from his earliest and his latest years. The very latest and, so he had promised himself, the last had been young enough to have been his granddaughter if he and his children had not been the human equivalents of those animals that his farmer-grandfather had called *shy breeders*. He, the personage in the upper room, had wanted only to exchange handwritten letters with the dark-haired woman. He foresaw a correspondence lasting for year after year in which two oddly matched persons came gradually to learn how closely they stood as readers of one another's handwriting, but in her third letter she had rebuked him for something that she claimed was inappropriate in an exchange between what she called an older writer and a younger reader. He had been so stung by her words that he had never afterwards dared to look at his copy of the offending letter or even of his subsequent hasty letter of apology. Each wrote once or twice more until she claimed not to have anything more worth writing about, which claim seemed to him absurd, although he believed he understood why she made it.

The subject-matter of the previous paragraphs may be thought of as being the contents of a handwritten or typewritten text composed by some or another fictional personage in some or another upper room of a house of two or, perhaps, three storeys. Most fiction has never been published, and even a published piece of fiction may be only a small part of a far-reaching unpublished text and an even farther-reaching collection of notes and jottings. The three paragraphs above, and several that will shortly appear below, may be thought of as reporting some of what might once have formed part of some or another published work of fiction if only they had been written at the time. Or, the same paragraphs may be thought of as a report of fictional events likely to have involved certain personages in a certain published work of fiction but in fictional places never mentioned in the published text and during fictional hours or days never reported by the narrator.

The first of the dark-haired females had taken his eye during his eighth year. She, being one of his classmates, would have been of the same age. She had a strange-sounding surname that he had never before heard, and he knew only the sound of it until thirty years later when he met a man of the same name and understood that it was French. If the boy had read the name before he had first heard it, he could never have known how to pronounce it. (Of course, as soon as he had first heard her surname, he visualised a written version of it, as he did with all words heard for the first time, but he never saw anywhere but in his mind his unwieldy private word and he felt sure that he had got it wrongly.) Words, both written and sounded, mattered greatly to him, even in his childhood, and his not knowing, for as long as he was interested in the dark-haired girl, how her surname was spelled was very much a part of her attractiveness. She arrived at his school at the beginning of the year and was gone before the end of it. He has class photographs for some of his years at primary school but not for her year, and yet he recalls her clearly. He has no memory of any words spoken between them but he can easily call to mind her scrutinising him, usually from the middle distance. Her face would hardly attract him nowadays, but he was stirred whenever she turned it towards him and stared as though trying to get his measure. Surely she knew that she was his girlfriend, in the language of that time and place; even if they had never spoken, she had surely learned as much from his own staring. Perhaps he had sent a message through one of her girlfriends, but such messages were always answered, even if with insults, and he would hardly have forgotten any hint that he had once received of her feelings towards him. And now he recalls that he once followed her homewards in order to learn where she lived. He recalls not so much his walking, one hot afternoon (in February or March?), out of the gravel schoolyard

by way of the gate that he had never before used and his
following the dark-haired girl at a distance along a road that led
in the opposite direction from his own neighbourhood, but his
overhearing his mother telling the woman from two houses away
what he had done and the two women then laughing together.
This puzzles him more than any other of his memories: that he
could have confided to his mother not only his having followed
the dark-haired girl but even his being interested in her.

His mother herself was dark-haired, as were four of her six
sisters. Three of those four had faintly olive skin. Once, as a
young man, he had studied his mother's family tree, hoping
to learn the source of the dark colouring, but the surnames
alone told him nothing; all were English, all of his mother's
eight great-grandparents having been born in either Devon
or Cumberland. He supposed there might have been dark-
haired descendants of the Celts still living in Devon in recent
centuries or that a gipsy from the Lake District might have
married into one of his ancestral families of small landholders
and tradesmen. In this, as in many other matters, he preferred
speculation to research.

His mother herself was dark-haired, as he seemed to have
learned for the first time one cold morning during his fifth year
and later to have forgotten until a certain cloudless afternoon
with a cool wind blowing while he was sometimes writing at his
desk and sometimes watching through his window the waving
of a clump of treetops in the middle distance. (The reader will
surely bring to mind some or another image formed earlier

while he or she read references to distant wings, upper storeys, sunlight falling on window-panes, and the like.) On the cold morning mentioned, he and she were together at the kitchen stove, she cooking porridge or toasting bread and he trying to warm himself. His two siblings were surely nearby, but he remembers only himself and his mother. All through his life, he was able to call up numerous memories from his fifth and his fourth years and some even from his third year, but his memory of the morning at the stove is the earliest memory in which a visual image of his mother appears. He has earlier memories of words spoken by her or of things done by her and memories of her as an unseen presence, but the image of the dark-haired woman at the stove is his earliest visual memory of his mother.

The woman at the stove wore a dressing-gown tied with a cord at the waist. Throughout his life, he has taken scant notice of clothes or fabrics or furnishings, but he believes he can recall the exact colours of the dressing-gown – he would call them indigo and silver-grey – and the exact feel of its silky texture. The dressing-gown belonged not to his mother but to his father. He was a minor public servant who neither drank nor smoked, and he and his family might have lived in frugal comfort except that he bet heavily on racehorses. He had never operated a bank account but carried a roll of banknotes always with him. After a series of winning bets, he would treat his wife and children to crayfish, blocks of chocolate, and what were called in those days family bricks of ice-cream and would peel off several banknotes from his roll and would tell his wife to buy with them something for herself and the children. His winning bets, however, were fewer than his losing bets, and during some of his lean periods, so to call them, he would place credit bets with bookmakers. After an especially lean period, three years after the cold morning mentioned above, he escaped from his gambling debts by quietly resigning from his public-service position, giving the minimum required notice to his landlord, and fleeing with his wife and children from the northern provincial city where he had lived for several years to his native district far away to the south-west.

The dressing-gown was one of several costly-seeming items that his father had bought from the proceeds of winning bets in the years before he had married. (He had been a bachelor until his mid-thirties.) Other such items were a bespoke three-piece suit that would have cost the equivalent of ten times his weekly earnings before his marriage; several pairs of gold cuff-links; a gold watch that his widow would finally sell, thirty years after his death, for a sum equal to her yearly income from the pension for the aged; and, of course, the dressing-gown, which was described earlier as having a silky feel and may well have been partly or wholly of silk.

His mother would have been wearing the dressing-gown because she had no dressing-gown of her own. She had been married in her eighteenth year, after she had been working for several years on the small farm belonging to her mother and her stepfather, who could seldom afford to pay her any wage. He, however, the chief character of these paragraphs of fiction, had not surmised until later years who had been the true owner of the gown. On the cold morning beside the stove, he considered the blue and silver gown his mother's property. She wore the gown often; his father never.

In his memories and in the connections between them, colour is always important. Nearly twenty years after the cold morning mentioned, he would try to write a poem to explain to himself why he had for long disliked the colour blue. While he was trying to write the poem, he supposed that the cause of his dislike was his never having been able during his first twenty years to fall in love with Mary, the mother of Jesus, even though he had felt continually obliged to do so. (Blue was traditionally associated with Mary, who was almost always depicted as wearing a blue robe or mantle.) He had never finished the poem, but before he had abandoned it he had recalled for perhaps the first time in twenty years, and in minute detail, the colours and the texture of the indigo and silver-grey dressing-gown and even the subtle interweaving of alternate strands of the two colours in each of the many approximate rectangles separating similarly shaped areas occupied by one or the other colour alone. He had recalled these details for the first time in many years in somewhat the same way that he would recall, many years later again and likewise for the first time in many years, and while he was at his desk in an upper room and preparing to write about certain dark-haired female persons, that his own mother had been dark-haired. And again, as on the earlier occasion, he seemed to feel what he had felt on the cold morning mentioned: as though his feelings came not from some mysterious part of his own person but from the

GERALD MURNANE

blue and silver strands of a fabric that he had not seen for sixty years and more.

On the cold morning mentioned he had decided, and for reasons that he could never afterwards recall, that his mother was not to be trusted. If he did not understand at the time how singular was his decision, he began to learn soon afterwards and went on learning throughout his life that it was singular indeed. He learned at the same time, however, what he ought to do and to say in order to seem to be a son who had never made any such decision about his mother. And she, his mother, whom he always suspected of knowing what he had decided on that cold morning, seemed to have learned what *she* ought to do and to say in order to seem what the two of them knew her not to be.

He had followed her home, so his mother had told her neighbour, in order to learn where she, the dark-haired girl, had lived, but at his desk who could say how many years afterwards, he could not be sure why he had walked out of the schoolyard through the gate that he had never before used and had walked ten or twenty paces behind her past the pepper trees marking the course of the creek and then over a timber bridge and into a network of streets where he had never previously been. He had never, in fact, learned exactly where she lived. It might have been enough for him to know that she lived in a district strange to him, or so he had surmised long afterwards when he recalled that the end of his adventure had been her turning around, soon after he had followed her across the bridge, and her staring at him until the face that he had previously considered pretty was creased and frowning, although perhaps not hostile. So he had surmised at his desk, but then he had got up and had stepped to the window. The sun had set, which allows *me* to surmise that the last rays of sunlight may have reached his window only a little while before, and while he had been writing his own version of the substance of this paragraph. He looked through the twilight towards one of the distant wings. He supposed it to be one of the wings occupied mostly by female personages, but he could not be sure. Here and there in the far wing, a window was already lit from within, and while he stared at one or another distant glow, he composed in his mind a sentence reporting that the boy turned back towards the bridge and the streets familiar to him from a concern that he had been about to disturb an existence hitherto untroubled.

She who had lived on the far side of the creek was named Barbara. (She was the first of four of that name who had attracted him during his first twenty years. Three of the four were dark-haired, although the one that he had most often in mind while he wrote fiction had pale hair.) After her came someone whose name he never learned. He could recall having seen her only once, and she was probably unaware of his existence. Like the first of the four Barbaras, she and her family moved into his suburb and then out again within a year, although this was not uncommon at a time when many families rented rather than owned their homes. When he saw her, she was with her two young brothers in the dusty front yard of their weatherboard house. After more than sixty years, he recalls only an approximation of her face but he can readily visualise what he believes to be the exact shade of the newly painted weatherboards behind her: something between grey and turquoise. He learned long ago not to struggle to recall her face but to call to mind first the bluish grey of the old timber house and then to hold the rare shade in focus, as it were, until he not only caught sight of some or another detail of clear, pale skin or dark eyebrows but felt what he supposed was something of the impression that the actual face had made on him long before, during the few minutes while he had observed it. He learned in time that this feeling was sometimes available to him even when he was unable to recall the face that had first given rise to it, and often in later years he needed only to call up an image of blue-grey weatherboards in order to feel again as though he was sauntering past a certain shabby house on a hot afternoon in the mid-1940s, in an inland provincial city, was staring at a girl of about his own age who was pushing repeatedly a worn rubber car-tyre suspended from a tree-branch and serving as a swing for one of her two younger brothers, and was waiting for her to turn so that he could see her face.

If, in the further reaches of some or another remote corridor in an immense house of two or, perhaps, three storeys, and behind some or another door that remains mostly closed but in sight of a window overlooking some or another tract of far-reaching landscape of mostly level grassy countryside with low hills or a line of trees in the distance, a certain man at his desk, on some or another day of sunshine with scattered clouds, were to spurn the predictable words and phrases of the many writers of fiction who have reported of this or that male character that he once fell in love with this or that female character, and if that same man, after striving as neither I, the author of this sentence, nor even the most discerning reader of the sentence, have or has striven nor will ever strive, in late afternoon, and at about the time when the rays of the declining sun might have caused the pane in the window of his room to seem to a traveller on a distant road like a spot of golden oil, had found in his heart, or wherever such things are to be found, the words best fitted to suggest what he seemed to have felt long before, on a certain hot afternoon, in a distant inland city, and whether he had simply kept those words in mind or whether he had actually written them, either as notes for a work of fiction that he might one day write or as part of an actual work of fiction, then I do not doubt that the words would have been to the effect that a certain boy, a mere child, while he watched unobserved a certain girl, a mere child, whose name he did not know and who had almost certainly never had sight of him, wished for the means to inform her that he was worthy of trust.

He passed the house of grey-blue weatherboards every day on his way to and from school, and he seems to remember that he saw her once or twice more, but he has no memory of the dark-haired girl's having looked even in his direction during the few months before she and her family moved whither he never knew. If she had attended his own school, matters might have gone differently between them, but he assumed that she walked every day to the distant state school by a route that did not cross his own. And yet he was not altogether content to remain unknown to her. The three or four unruly children in the shabby house next to his went also to the state school, and he recalls his confiding to two of them, a brother and a sister of about his own age, that the dark-haired girl in the grey-blue house was his girlfriend. What should have followed, according to the customs of that time and place, was the two confidants' hurrying to tell the girl what they hoped would unsettle or even annoy her and afterwards bringing back to the boyfriend an exaggerated or false report meant to affect him likewise. When, after several days, he had heard nothing from the children his neighbours, he waylaid them and asked for details. He took their vague answers for lies and surmised that they had forgotten even to approach the dark-haired girl. He made no further effort to reach the girl, although he looked out for her whenever he passed the blue-grey house. He seems to recall as his chief regret that he had not enabled her to experience what would have been for him strangely satisfying: an awareness of the esteem of someone altogether unknown.

What I wrote in the seventh section of this work of fiction is no more than the merest beginnings of an account of the matter of point-of-view in fiction. During the years when I supposed that the writing of fiction was a craft and that a writer of fiction was obliged to strive continually to improve his or her craftsmanship, I read closely the first edition and then, nearly ten years later, the revised and expanded second edition of a bulky book almost wholly given over to a study of point-of-view in fiction, although the author hardly ever used that term, perhaps because it seemed to make too readily accessible a field of study that he, a professor in an American university, had made his life's work. I have not looked into either book for nearly twenty years, but I still recall my studying several charts or diagrams towards the rear of the book, trying to learn from them the subtle distinctions between the many possible kinds of fictional narration. I found the charts or diagrams intimidating, but not nearly as much so as an arrangement of several concentric circles criss-crossed by six or seven axes and containing, at close intervals all around their circumference, the titles of fifty and more so-called classics of English literature, which arrangement I saw reproduced nearly thirty years ago in *The Times Literary Supplement*, which I used to get by airmail from England during the years when I supposed that a writer of fiction was obliged to be aware of the sorts of fiction being published in distant countries. The arrangement, as I call it, had been reproduced from a book that was reviewed respectfully and at great length in the surrounding columns. The book, which had been published by the press of a famous English university, was the English translation of a work by a renowned German scholar. His field, so to call it, was narratology, which was a word I had never previously come across. Although I could make little sense of the review, I found myself admiring the concentric circles and the axes and the dense array of fictional titles in the illustration. I got from the illustration a sense that the writing of fiction was not only a craft but that the endless-seeming difficulties that I experienced while planning and writing fiction might have been inevitable, given the complexity of my task. The narratologist, so to call him, had claimed to discover certain standards for measuring such matters as the seeming nearness of a fictional narrator to his or her characters; the seeming awareness of the fictional narrator that he or she is also a writer; or the amount that the fictional narrator claims to know over and beyond what the characters collectively know. These and several other supposedly measurable matters were represented on the illustrated diagram by the axes that transected the concentric circles. (I long ago forgot what the circles themselves were intended to represent.) The title of each of the fifty and more so-called classics was positioned where it was after the renowned scholar had presumably pored over the text (the original English or a German translation? I cannot recall) in a state of heightened alertness and with no more than a reader's sensitivity to enable him to register each precise calibration on the several subtle narratological scales.

Whereas I found useful the books by the American professor and borrowed from them several terms that I still sometimes use when talking or writing about fictional narration, I was inclined to scoff at the German scholar's chart, which put me in mind of some or another inscrutable calendar or sky-map from a civilisation long since vanished. And yet, after seeming to have forgotten for nearly thirty years the concentric circles and the diametric axes and the book-titles positioned all around like tiny asteroids, I recalled them today and was compelled to mention them in this piece of fiction. At first, I supposed I had done so for no other purpose than to startle the undiscerning reader who believes that a work of fiction contains little more than reports of so-called characters, of what those characters do and say and think, and of the scenery, so to call it, in the background. But then I called to mind some of the writers of fiction in the house of two or, perhaps, three storeys where much of the action, so to call it, of this work of fiction takes place. Those personages, if I know anything about them, might have looked, long ago, into the American's books and might even have used occasionally one or another of the American's technical terms when speaking about their own or others' writing but would surely have never heard of the German or of his book. If pressed to give an account of their working methods, they might fall back on the word *instinct* or on equally vague phrases such as *the rightness of things*, *concern for detail*, or *eloquent simplicity*. And yet, if I were to put in front of those personages a diagram not unlike a spider's web, with titles of books and obscure technical terms superimposed on each of its many zones, and if I were to ask the personages whether each of their own works of fiction might be susceptible to the sort of analysis that had given rise to the diagram, I believe that each of them, fictional personages though they are, would concur with myself, the narrator of the work in which they have their existence. I believe that each of them would admit that he has sometimes got up from his desk late on some or another afternoon and has stepped to the window and has looked through the glass at a view of mostly level grassy countryside, hopeful that someone passing along a distant road and looking in his, the fictional personage's direction, would see not a window of a house of two or, perhaps, three storeys but something as unlooked for as a spot of golden oil.

A certain personage from among those mentioned in the last sentences of the previous section might well be at work now, in whichever room he happens to occupy, on his own version of what follows.

On a certain afternoon in one of the first months of his fifteenth year, and while he was travelling in the grimy rear compartment of a second-class carriage of an electric train from the inner suburb where he attended school to the outer suburb where he lived, which two suburbs were south-east of the capital city where he had been born and were about ten kilometres apart, he noticed that a certain dark-haired girl of about his own age in a certain corner of the compartment was the same girl who had sat in the same corner on the previous afternoon. He remembers nothing of what he did or thought on either of the afternoons mentioned, but he assumes that he looked so often and so intently at the girl that she became aware of his looking, even though he had supposed that he was looking in a way that would not take her notice.

Long afterwards, he would sometimes ask himself why that one face from among the many faces of the many schoolgirls that he saw each day – why that one face had provoked him not only to look but to look in such a way as would cause him to believe, during the following weeks and months, that she whose face it was had learned already about him much more than he could have hoped to learn about her even if he had looked at her continually during the time they were together. It may have been that the girl in the railway compartment looked as a certain other dark-haired girl might have looked seven or eight years after he had last seen her in a dusty front yard of a provincial city. It may have been that the contrast between the black hair of the girl in the railway compartment and the zone of warm colour around her cheekbones recalled for him not only the last detail remaining to him of the earlier girl – a black eyebrow above a flushed cheek – but the red-stemmed green leaves of a sycamore tree, the yellow-grey dust of a front yard, the blue-grey weatherboards of a house-front, and some of the earliest intimations he would afterwards remember that the drab or the everyday, so to call them, are mere signs of another order of things. But this line of thinking led him further away from understanding how a face alone could have had such an influence on him and not even a face but a few details of a face. And while these matters exercised him, he recalled that he had never, in fact, seen her head of dark hair. Only a few strands curved past her ears from beneath the wide-brimmed, dome-topped hat of her school uniform. (Surely a bunch of hair was visible at the nape of her neck although he never afterwards recalled any sight of it.) There seemed no answer to his question.

A few strands of hair and a small area of skin of a certain colour had started him on a detailed mental enterprise that occupied much of his free time for two years.

It might well be possible to compose the better part of a book-length work of fiction by drawing on the details of what I called in the previous paragraph a mental enterprise. The enterprise, so to call it, might well consist of the chief character's foreseeing his courting the dark-haired girl at an appropriate time in the future and afterwards, at decent intervals, their becoming engaged, their marrying and honeymooning, and finally, their becoming the parents of a large family. All these details might well go towards the making of a work of fiction, but the sort of writer that I have mostly in mind while I write *this* work of fiction has mostly in mind while he writes not the published or the readily publishable but what lies behind, or to the side of, or deep beneath the subject-matter, whether actual or seeming. This being so, the young man, hardly more than a boy, who might be supposed to have exchanged glances for two years with a certain dark-haired young woman, hardly more than a girl, will not be reported in these paragraphs as living in his mind a fictional future with himself and herself as its chief characters but merely as preparing himself to approach her and to speak to her.

There was one other possible reason for his being drawn to her, although he became aware of it only after they had been exchanging glances for some weeks, so that it could not have explained his first, strong interest in her. In all the time while they shared the same railway compartment, she made no effort to encourage or embolden him, or none that he recognised as such. A routine had soon developed between them. They seemed agreed that their eyes should not meet for more than an instant. When he first boarded the train, he would look directly at her and she at him, but each would then look immediately away. At intervals thereafter, he would look around the compartment as though lost in thought but always so as to take in the sight of her reading in her corner seat. If she kept her eyes on her book, he might observe her for a few moments, but if she looked up, their unspoken rules obliged each to look elsewhere at once. What I called just now their rules never seemed to him harsh or unjust. What he might have called her good looks put him rather in awe of her, and it probably seemed appropriate to him that she should be difficult of access. Long afterwards, he supposed that if she had once smiled at him he could not have brought himself to smile in return but would have gone on with his patient, earnest campaign.

She made no seeming effort to encourage him, but on one occasion she responded in kind to a move that he had made. That was on the afternoon when he set out to have her learn his name. His given name and his surname were both somewhat uncommon, and so he printed both boldly on the cover of a schoolbook that he took home regularly. What he planned had to wait for an evening when the seats in their compartment were all occupied and no one stood in his way to prevent him from standing directly above her corner seat. While she herself was reading, he took out from his bag, which was resting in the

luggage-rack at the height of his head, the book with his name on
its cover. He looked into the book for a few minutes and then, as if
trying to memorise something from its pages, closed his book and
tucked it between his chest and his upper arm so that his name
would be visible if she looked upwards. He had to repeat these
actions twice, and each time a little more emphatically, before he
saw from the sides of his eyes that she had read his name.

He had wanted only that *she* should learn *his* name. He had
thought this would make a little less abrupt and startling his
eventually confronting her and introducing himself; he had not
expected her to do what she did next.

She carried always an elegant-looking leather case that rested
across her knees while she sat in the train. He had sometimes
entertained a preposterous daydream: that she would leave the
case behind her in the train one afternoon or would drop it in
the grass beside the railway line when she fled homewards from
the scene of a terrible traffic accident. (He and she left the train
at the same station, although they set out in opposite directions
thereafter.) He, of course, would find the case, would find her
address inside, and would later return the case to her home,
which would have given him the opportunity to talk to her at
last. Before returning the case, however, he would spend several
hours examining every item it contained, stroking and feeling
the items that she herself handled so often, and trying to learn
from the way she had stacked or arranged the items what were
some of her whims and preferences. Above all, he would read
whatever was written in her own hand in her school exercise-

books. He would read aloud every sentence of every essay that she herself had composed. He would learn from the oddities of her handwriting and from the choice of words and the patterns and stresses in her prose a sort of knowledge that he could never hope to learn from mere conversation.

After she had looked for a few moments in the direction of the book resting under his arm, she unfastened her case and took out an exercise-book. She looked into the book as though wanting to check what was her homework for that evening, and then she closed the book and placed it with its front cover upwards on top of her case, which was now closed again. He had been tense and uneasy while he was displaying his own name for her inspection, and when he had understood that she was showing him her name he became even more so. His eyesight was sound, and the railway compartment was so well lit by afternoon sunlight that he could have read the fine print of a newspaper if she had rested such a thing in front of her, but he struggled to make out her name, even though her handwriting was of average neatness. His first impulse was to look away, as he would certainly have looked away if he had been walking behind her one afternoon down the ramp from the railway platform and if a gust of wind had lifted her skirt from her thighs. He might have looked eagerly at the name on the exercise-book if he had been spying on her, but he was not ready to have her make it so freely available to him. He became somewhat calmer after he had made out her surname, which was not an uncommon name, but he became agitated again when he could not decide what was her given name. The word was of medium length with its letters boldly formed in blue ink, but he could not recognise the word. For all his confusion, he had no wish to cause her the least anxiety, and after what he considered an appropriate interval he looked away as though he had easily interpreted the only written message she would ever send him, whereupon she returned the book to her leather case.

It might have been better for him if her given name had appeared as a blur, but he had read it as *D-a-t-h-a-r*, which he felt sure was a misreading. He did not need to consult any books of girls' names to know that no girl-child in the English-speaking parts of the world had ever been named *Dathar*, although he sometimes thought her mother might have belonged to some or another dark-haired Slavic minority group in whose language *dathar* meant *fair of face* or *blessed by fortune*. Mostly, he felt as though he had failed an elementary test that anyone in his situation should have passed with ease: as though he was henceforth disqualified from thinking of himself as having a girlfriend, given that he could not even read her name after she had exposed it to him.

He had felt, on several occasions during the third decade of his life, that he was about to experience what was mostly called in those years a nervous breakdown. On all but one of these occasions, he had sought no help and had either avoided the breakdown by some or another means or had experienced the breakdown and had survived it, although he could never afterwards have said which of those two was the correct version of events. On one of those occasions, he had consulted a psychiatrist who had advised him, among other things, to meet weekly in his, the psychiatrist's rooms, with six or seven others of his patients, all males, in the expectation that their discussions would serve as what was called in those years *group therapy* and would result in each person's either avoiding the nervous breakdown that he was threatened with or recovering soon from that which he had recently suffered. He, the likely chief character of any further version of these already fictional events, joined the group for five or six weeks but then wrote to the psychiatrist explaining why he would no longer attend, his chief reason being that the men in the group mostly gossiped when they should have been confessing their problems and asking for advice. Of all that was talked about in the group he recalled long afterwards only an account by a certain man who was married and a father of his becoming interested, when he had been a young man and hardly more than a boy, in a female person of about his own age who was one of a small group who waited every morning at the same suburban bus stop. He who was hardly more than a boy had glanced often at her who was hardly more than a girl, and she had glanced almost as often at him. After the two had glanced thus for several months, the young man, hardly more than a boy, resolved to speak to the young woman, hardly more than a girl, although he dreaded doing so. On morning after morning, he walked from his home to the bus stop rehearsing in his mind a certain few words that he intended that morning to say to the young woman, which words were about the weather or the likelihood of the bus's arriving on time. On morning after morning, he could not bring himself to utter the words in the hearing of the young woman. Then, on a certain morning, he forced himself to stand beside the young woman and to deliver his rehearsed words in her direction. He could never recall afterwards whether or not he had delivered the words; he could recall only his waking on the grass beside the bus stop and being told by the concerned persons around him that he had fainted shortly beforehand.

Several members of the group in the psychiatrist's rooms had been amused by the man's account while several others had seemed to suppose that the man had been exaggerating and had not actually fainted at the bus stop, but the likely chief character, as I called him above, not only believed every detail of the man's account but asked him whether or not the young woman, hardly more than a girl, had been one of the concerned persons surrounding him while he recovered from his fainting fit and whether or not he and she had spoken to one another on subsequent mornings at the bus stop and had become friends. The man replied that he had been too ashamed to look into the faces of any of the concerned persons and that he had returned home at once and had never afterwards taken a bus to work but had walked each morning far out of his way to a railway station. The chief character, as I call him, would have liked to tell the man who had fainted the story of his, the chief character's, dealing silently for two years with the young woman, hardly more than a girl, whose name he had once misread as *Dathar*, but he did not trust the other men in the group to comment honestly on what he might have told them.

If he had not mistrusted most of the men who met in the psychiatrist's rooms, the chief character of the paragraphs hereabouts might have told them not that he had fainted away on the afternoon when he had spoken, or had tried to speak, for the first time to the young woman, hardly more than a girl, that he had looked at for two years but that he had never been able afterwards to recall anything of the occasion. He could readily recall during the remainder of his life the events leading up to the occasion. A small child had misbehaved in the compartment where he and the young woman travelled, and he had resolved to walk beside the young woman after they had left the train and to remark on the child's antics. (One possible reason for his having waited for so long before speaking was his being unable to compose what would have been his opening remarks. He could never have merely greeted her or commented on the weather. He felt obliged to impress her from the very first with wit or humour.) He could recall afterwards, with some difficulty, his walking beside the young woman for a short distance before they took their separate ways homewards. And given that the young woman smiled at him when he entered the railway compartment on the following afternoon and that later he sat beside her when a seat had become available and that they talked together during the remainder of their journey, he could not doubt that he had communicated with her in some way or another during the few minutes that he could never afterwards recall. But whether he had said something witty or humorous or something banal or whether he had forced from his constricted throat only some or another friendly sound he would never know. He had certainly not fainted away as had the young man at the bus stop, but part of him had seemingly been numbed or had ceased to function.

As I reported in the previous paragraph, the young woman smiled at the young man as soon as he had stepped into her compartment on the afternoon following his attempt to speak to her, and he and she afterwards talked together. Had she not smiled, the young man would have assumed that no words from him had reached her on the previous afternoon and would merely have exchanged glances with her as before. He and she talked together at last, but the reader should not have in mind an image of two young persons chatting amicably and being at ease with one another. Perhaps the young woman was at ease and was amicably disposed towards the young man, but he was so ill at ease that he was afterwards unable to recall any more than two sentences spoken by the young woman from all that she had said to him during five or ten minutes of conversation on ten or, perhaps, fifteen weekday afternoons before the afternoon when they said goodbye to one another as usual while they walked down the ramp from the railway platform and then went their separate ways, even while he, the young man, had decided that he wanted no more to do with the young woman.

He, whether the reader perceives him as a character in a work of fiction being written by a personage in an upper room of a house of two or, perhaps, three storeys or as a fictional personage in a fictional setting not yet written about or merely as a character in this present work of fiction – he, however he may be perceived, was afterwards able to recall only two items from all that the young woman must surely have talked about during the two or three weeks when he and she had talked together at last. The first of the two items was her given name, which was Darlene. He surely told her during their first conversation that he had been unable to make out her given name on the afternoon when she had placed her exercise-book in his view, but he surely did not tell her that he had thought of her during the previous year as bearing the absurd name of *Dathar*. The second of the two items was a question that she asked him on the last afternoon when he and she spoke together, which question will be reported later in this work of fiction. Whatever else he had learned about the young woman he afterwards forgot, if he had even absorbed it during their time together, so that she seems to him today not a person that he once dealt with in the world where I sit writing these sentences but an inscrutable image-person whose appearance was derived from a certain dark-haired young woman, hardly more than a girl, that he saw often in a certain railway compartment: an image-person who might have been the chief character of a complicated daydream-world that the girl in the railway compartment could never have guessed at and who later became one of the chief characters in a certain published work of fiction in which she has a different name from the name of the young woman mentioned in the paragraphs and is reported as behaving somewhat differently.

GERALD MURNANE

At some time during every day, I like to walk in the grounds that
I see often from my upstairs window but have hardly begun to
explore. The reader should not suppose from my having used
the word *grounds* just now what I supposed during the first
years when I frequented this singular building. I used then to
suppose that the extensive formal parks and lawns and lakes and
flower-beds, together with the labyrinths of paths and walkways
connecting them, would have ended abruptly in every direction,
and at some considerable distance from the building, in a high
fence or a wall or hedge, on the further side of which would have
been the nearest paddocks of the mostly level grassy countryside
that seems to surround building and grounds on all sides and
seems to be crossed at long intervals by roads where sunlight
flashes occasionally in the late afternoon from the windscreen of
some or another car or truck too far away to be seen or heard,
and seems to extend far beyond the low hills or the lines of
trees on the horizon. In fact, I have never come across any such
fence or wall or hedge. I mostly stroll without purpose in the
grounds around this mansion, so to call it, but I have sometimes
walked directly away from the building, wanting to learn how far
I might travel while still feeling myself in sight of a few at least of
the sumless windows behind me. Not only did I never come up
against any seeming boundary, but I was never able to decide,
at the furthest point of my excursion, whether the mostly level
grass and the scattered trees around me were still part of the
estate that included the tall house where I belonged for the time
being or whether I had strayed across some unmarked border

64

into the countryside that had always seemed, when I looked towards it from my upper window, beyond the reach of a person writing for hour after hour at a desk.

I mostly stroll without purpose, as I wrote above, and yet I seem to be drawn often to one particular sort of place. In several level areas within sight of one or another wing of the house, so to call it, I find myself seemingly ensnared for the time being among a number of pebbled paths forming a series of concentric circles separated each from the other by a box hedge reaching no higher than my thighs. From an upper window of the nearest wing, the paths and the hedges between might appear as one of those carefully planned and tended mazes where persons become truly lost among dense green barriers higher than themselves and where they cry out to be led back to the outside world, so to call it. Never, on any path among the dwarf-hedges, have I ceased to know where I stood in relation to this towering building in the one direction and the mostly level and far-reaching countryside in the other. And yet, I have been sometimes able to experience, while I supposed myself trapped for the time being in a whorl of topiary even though in sight of safety – I have been sometimes able to experience what I suppose to be the pleasurable confusion of a certain sort of reader of a certain sort of fiction.

Somewhere in both the first and the later edition of his book, the American scholar mentioned earlier uses the expression *double-voicing* to denote the technique by which the narrator of a work of fiction is able to seem to report a series of events while

at the same time seeming to report the thoughts and feelings of
some or another character involved in the events. The technique
has been used by numerous narrators, but the undiscerning
reader of this narrative may still be in need of an example.

*Nick rubbed his eye. There was a big bump coming up. He would
have a black eye, all right. It ached already. That son of a crutting
brakeman.*

The four sentences and the exclamation above are part of some
or another work of fiction by Ernest Hemingway. A person
reading the sentences with alertness should hear, as it were,
two voices, one voice being that of the narrator and the other
being that of the character Nick. In the first sentence, only
the voice of the narrator can be heard. In the second, third,
and fourth sentences, that same voice is heard again. In those
three sentences, however, the voice of the narrator reports
not only his own observations but sensations and insights of
the character himself, and when these two are reported the
language seems not only the narrator's but partly that of the
character. The discerning reader might even notice a gradual
change in the viewpoint from sentence to sentence. The first
sentence reports only what might be seen of the character.
Later sentences move more closely, as it were, towards the
character's own viewpoint, and the final exclamation seems so
much in keeping with the character that it might have been
enclosed within quotation marks. By this time, the narrator

who seemed, only moments earlier, to be addressing us in his own voice has seemed to fall silent.

I would estimate that rather more than half the fiction published during my lifetime is written from a point of view hardly different from that of the passage quoted above and seems to be told by a narrator claiming to know all that is known to the chief character but not much more. By this I mean that if the narrator were reporting the visit of the chief character to a certain hotel, he or she (the narrator) would not usually inform the reader that the hotel had been the site, a hundred years before, of the founding of a certain political party or of a notorious murder if the chief character was unaware of such matters. Not only have I read much fiction of the sort quoted but I have myself sometimes written such fiction and not wanted afterwards to repudiate it. This sort of fiction provides its readers with an experience not unlike what I felt when I stood confused among the concentric box hedges and gravel paths. I was not lost or in any sort of danger. Even if I had not been able to plot a path outwards through the hedges, I could have scrambled over them or through them and could have got back to my room whenever I chose. For as long as I limited my thinking, however; for as long as I observed what I supposed were the conventions of gardens and their designers; for as long as I felt bound to walk only on designated pathways and forbidden from breaking through even a miniature hedge, then I seemed truly a captive of the artifice and of whoever had designed it, even though I could look away at any time from the petty labyrinth and outwards towards the far-reaching countryside or upwards towards this massive building and its numerous windows.

I have not wanted to repudiate any fiction of mine the narrator of which has the viewpoint described above, but I have wanted, for almost as long as I have been a writer of fiction, to secure for myself a vantage-point from which each of the events reported in a work of fiction such as this present work, and each of the personages mentioned in the work, might seem, at one and the same time, a unique and inimitable entity impossible to define or to classify but also a mere detail in an intricate scheme or design. I might have written instead of the previous sentence that I have for long wanted to call into being a fictional narrator by definition more knowledgeable and more trustworthy than a personage such as myself, the narrator of this present work.

I have been sometimes dissatisfied with the sort of narration in which the thoughts and feelings of the chief character alone are reported. ('Nick rubbed his eye...') I have sometimes felt concerned that such fiction diminishes the importance of the narrator. The undiscerning reader of such fiction might well suppose himself or herself merely to be witnessing one after another event, so to call it, in the life, so to call it, of the chief character in almost the way that the viewer of a film supposes himself or herself to be witnessing actuality, so to call it. And yet, this sort of fiction gives to its reader an experience far richer and more satisfying than is offered by the spurious sort of fiction that seems to lack a narrator.

Was it thirty or forty years ago when I first tried to read the only work that I have tried to read by a certain author from Latin America who was later awarded the Nobel Prize for Literature? I long ago forgot the title of the book that I once tried to read. I had first learned about the book when I read a most favourable review of it in *The Times Literary Supplement*. I had paid my bookseller of those days a sum that was for me substantial so that she could have a single copy of the book sent to me by sea from England. I began to read the book with much expectation but was puzzled and dissatisfied before I had read twenty pages.

I have confessed already in these pages to being an ignorant and gullible reader. Thirty or forty years ago, I was even more ignorant and more gullible. After I had read the first twenty pages of the acclaimed work of fiction and had got no satisfaction from them, I was inclined to blame myself and my lack of skill as a reader. Even so, I read closely again the pages that had failed to satisfy me and further pages still, looking into the text itself for a possible cause of my dissatisfaction. I suspect that I had not previously studied the narrative technique of any work of fiction. I would have been well aware of the presence of many a narrator while I read but unaware of his or her technique or of its being only one of many that might have been used. In spite of my ignorance, I was quick to recognise that the fiction of the celebrated Latin American lacked any sort of narrative presence. I would have been hesitant thirty or forty years ago to blame or condemn the famous author but I long since decided that the author of a text lacking a narrative presence is guilty of posturing or, more likely, of incompetence.

What I read on the first page of the book mentioned was a monologue, and an undistinguished monologue at that. Someone who might have been male or female and of any age – someone was responsible for an uninterrupted outpouring. No, the author of the text in front of my eyes had written a report intended to persuade me that I was privy to – what were they? – the thoughts, the mutterings, the memories, or the daydreams of an utterly unknown thinker, mutterer, rememberer, or daydreamer. (However ignorant and gullible I might have been at the time, I could never have supposed the monologue, as I call it, to be any sort of purported text, as though the author of the book in front of me was quoting from the writings of one or another of his characters, so to call them. Even the least-skilled of writers could have composed something more readable than the unvarying wordage in front of me.)

After I had read a certain number of densely printed pages, I came to a gap in the text. After the gap came another body of text hardly different from the first, and even the reader that I was at that time began to resent the lack of information provided. Was the second monologue to be attributed to the same young or old, male or female thinker or mutterer or rememberer or daydreamer who had been responsible for the first? Or, was I now reading the presumed thoughts or whatever of quite another personage? Even the reader that I was at the time could see that the rhythms and the grammar of the second monologue differed in no way from those of the first. Perhaps the gap in the text was intended to denote an interval of fictional time.

(The previous sentence happens to be the culmination of a series of sentences illustrating once again the form of narration exemplified by the passage that I quoted earlier from Ernest Hemingway. Quite without meaning to do so, I, as narrator, composed the series in order to point up the situation of my chief character, in this case my younger self. My having done so should demonstrate the usefulness of this mode of narration and even, perhaps, what might be called its naturalness.)

The reader of these pages will hardly need to be told that a third unattributed monologue or, rather, a third written report of an unattributed monologue followed the second. I cannot recall how many such reports I read before I gave up reading the highly praised book, but I recall that I looked ahead in order to satisfy myself that the hundreds of pages yet to be read comprised nothing else but report after report of monologue after monologue from some or another nameless thinker, or mutterer, or rememberer or daydreamer.

At some time when I was trying to read the highly praised book, I learned from the publisher's advertisement on the dust-jacket that the novel, so to call it, was written in a *spiral of time*. Perhaps, being gullible and ignorant, I decided that a great deal had now been explained; that I was at fault for not having recognised the invisible whorled structure that gave coherence and meaning to what I had found incoherent and meaningless. Perhaps I even searched for evidence of time's being arranged spiral-wise in the jumble of text. (I surely understood at the time that a close study of events and places and persons referred to in each monologue could have told me who was the presumed speaker of each and when, in the time-sequence of the whole work, each speaker could have been presumed to have delivered his or her outpouring. But I was just as surely hindered from doing so by the fact that each of the monologues, as I call them, was made up of the same unrelenting prose. Authors of fiction purporting to come from a medley of voices are seldom skilful enough to compose a distinctive prose for each supposed speaker.) If I did thus search, I could hardly have found anything to justify the publisher's absurd claim. I recall only that I put the book away unread and have never since looked into it or felt any desire to read any other work by the celebrated author.

In an earlier paragraph of this section, I tried to compare my situation among the circular paths in the grounds of this building with the situation of a reader content to know in detail about only the chief character of a work of fiction. Elsewhere in this section, I tried to describe a sort of narration that I could wish to achieve and a sort of narrator that I could wish to become. Am I being too fanciful if I end this section by describing myself as standing again among the paths and the box-hedges but this time being reminded of a bewildering diagram in a book of several hundred pages on the subject of narratology – a diagram of concentric circles and diametrical axes – and regretting that I, a fictional personage myself, have never yet seemed a part of such complexity? Or, should I simply report my pleasant confusion when I look away from the hedges and paths and upwards towards the nearest wing of this building and the window of the room in which these words are being written at this very time?

I am writing again about a supposed author, as I might call him: someone at a desk in some or another room at no great distance from here. He is struggling, if I know anything about him, to compose a few pages of fiction based on, or relating to, or derived from, or inspired by a few weeks that he has never been able to recall. Those were the weeks during his seventeenth year when he sat beside a certain young woman, hardly more than a girl, in a suburban railway train and when they talked together for perhaps ten minutes on every weekday afternoon. If the supposed author, so to call him, believes that a writer of fiction is obliged to explain why his characters, so to call them, behave as they are reported as behaving in his fiction, then he has much to explain about his chief character, a young man, hardly more than a boy, who talked for a few weeks with the young woman mentioned in the previous sentence. He, the supposed author, has to explain, for example, why his chief character had previously travelled regularly for two years in the same railway compartment with the young woman and had glanced often in her direction but had made no attempt to speak to her. Alternatively, if the supposed author feels no obligation to explain what might be called the motives of those who might be called his characters, then his readers, whoever they might be, are free to devise their own explanations. One such reader, for example, might suppose that the chief character, although he would never have used such terms, had always preferred fictional personages to actual personages. That same reader might suppose further that the chief character, soon after he had first exchanged glances with a certain young female person in a railway compartment, had met up with a certain fictional female personage, so to call her. The reader might further suppose that this personage, on a certain afternoon during her fictional life and when she was still a young woman, hardly more than a girl, had met up with a certain fictional male personage, a young man and hardly more than a boy. The lives of the two fictional personages had then seemed to go forward not as the lives of actual persons go forward but as the lives of characters in works of fiction are enabled to go forward, which is to say that the deeds and words and thoughts of the personages seemed not to occur in what is commonly called *time* but in what was called earlier in this work the *narrative dimension*. In that dimension, events, so to call them, that might have occupied a year of actual time, so to call it, are reported in a single paragraph whereas the contents of a few moments might need for their full appraisal a chapter that might detain the reader for an hour and might have occupied the writer for a week. In short, while scant details might be said to have been noted from the years when the two young fictional personages chatted in railway compartments or on outings together, details abounded from their later years. Their intimate conversations were transcribed, as it were. Sentences and whole paragraphs were quoted, as it were, from the letters that they wrote during their brief times apart. And, given that these two personages were far from being characters in an actual text, their behaviour was explained in minute detail. And the subject-matter, so to call it, of this fiction-in-the-mind, as it might be called, included the courtship of the two personages, their engagement, their marriage, their honeymoon, and year after year of their life together as husband and wife and parents.

During a certain few moments of a certain afternoon, the chief character of a conjectured piece of fiction spoke for the first time, or so it would have been reported in the piece of fiction, with another character, a young female character whose name he had once misread as *Dathar*. He, the chief character, could never afterwards recall what he had said to the young female character while they were walking down the ramp from the railway station after having travelled together in silence in the same railway compartment during the previous fifteen minutes. Nor could he afterwards recall what, if anything, she had said to him in reply, but after she had smiled at him when he entered her railway compartment on the following afternoon he had sat beside her as soon as a seat had become available and had talked with her.

He and she, the characters or personages or whatever else the reader may consider them, had talked thus together during the next few weeks. Their conversations had lasted for a total time of about three hours. Given that a great deal of what he heard from her would have answered questions that had occurred to him during the previous two years – what siblings had she? where had she spent her early childhood? where did she go for her holidays? what were her favourite books? what were her hobbies? – he found it strange in later years that he failed to recall not only her answers to such questions but even his posing the questions. In later years he would sometimes feel such unease when alone with some or another female person that he could afterwards recall nothing of the experience, but he was never able to believe that he had been stricken in the presence of Darlene, as he would have learned to call her, with the sort of apprehension that overcame him in the presence of those others. The fact that he willingly met up with her on day after day for several weeks argues against his having been wary or uneasy with her as he was sometimes wary or uneasy in later years with certain female persons, dark-haired or otherwise. The preceding is the sort of sentence that might appear often among the notes made by an author committed to explaining the behaviour of his or her characters, so to call them. If I were reporting the strange forgetfulness of the chief characters of these paragraphs, I would report no more than what is reported in such as the following paragraph.

From all that she had surely said to him during three hours or more, he later recalled only one sentence or, rather, the substance of one sentence. He had never forgotten her having asked him one afternoon, while the train was approaching the suburb where they both lived, whether he was interested in – did she say *films* or *movies* or *pictures*?

Among the authors who have never been committed to explaining the behaviour, so to call it, of characters, so to call them, are the authors who are committed to reporting a certain sort of detail. This is the detail that occurs unexpectedly and unbidden and as though meant to occupy a blank or an absence in the place where images of details or even of words or phrases or sentences appear to writers of fiction. A certain sort of writer, after having written all that could seemingly be written about a character unable to recall more than three words that might have been uttered by a certain dark-haired young woman – a certain sort of writer might have stared at those words themselves where they appeared at the end of a short paragraph; might have heard the words seeming to sound repeatedly in his mind; and might have seemed to feel the beginnings of an unease or discomfort or distaste seemingly connected with the words until there appeared in place of the words detail after detail of the sort reported in the following paragraphs.

If I know anything about him and his struggles to write fiction while recalling not seeming facts but absences, lacks, lacunae, he would sooner or later have decided that her asking him about films, or whatever was her actual word, had decided the future of their friendship, so to call it, and would have come as a relief to him. Since the afternoon when they had begun, at last, to talk together, he would have struggled during their absences from one another, and perhaps even during their brief conversations, to form some or another series of mental images linking their present unpredictable circumstances with the well-established series of future events that had seemed to him, since they had first looked at one another, their inevitable future. In short, he would have struggled to foresee how a young woman, hardly more than a girl, and a young man, hardly more than a boy, she in a fetching uniform of brown with blue and gold trimmings and he in plain grey with a cap of faded blue – how those two could bear to spend year after year engaged in trivial matters while knowing all the while that a notable future awaited them: that they would be in due course boyfriend and girlfriend, an engaged couple, a married couple, a pair of honeymooners, and, finally, the parents of numerous children. His relief would have come from her having given away some part, at least, of the future that she foresaw for the two of them. Her question had told him that they were not merely to talk at length to one another by telephone or in one another's lounge-room; nor would they write long letters to one another. He had understood at once where her question about films was meant to lead them, and he had understood at once that he would not be led in that direction. She had answered in part his unasked question: how could she and he endure the many dull years before their dream-future overtook them? On many a Friday or Saturday evening they would sit together in the Plaza or the Paramount, which were the two cinemas in the suburb adjoining their own.

Did he never, while they talked in the train, enjoy for a little the awareness that an actual future was now before him; that he could rest for the time being from his strenuous day-dreaming and watch actual events unfolding around him and her? He recalls no such pleasant interludes. Words, words that had him constantly adjusting his assumptions of two years past, were issuing from the mouth of someone who had been during all that time as silent as a statue and had seemed to speak only when he had willed her or, rather, her image to speak what he had composed on her behalf. Did he never, while they talked in the train, try to persuade himself that his two-years-long dream had come true: that he had now gained the friendship of a flesh-and-blood person and had no longer to court a creature of his own devising? At his desk in the house of many windows, he recalls no such efforts. All he recalls is his having decided, whether soon or late during the few weeks while they talked, that his earlier state had been preferable to his later; that he may well have been in love with Dathar but he could never be in love with Darlene.

Their suburb was a new suburb that had been a few years previously a cluster of industrial buildings surrounded by swampy paddocks and bisected by a railway line. His and her families were unusual, the parents having paid deposits on cheap weatherboard houses after having lived for years in rented cottages in inner suburbs. Most families in the suburb were young couples, as they were called, with two or three small children. Hardly any householder owned a car. Buses carried women to the shopping centre in the adjoining suburb, families to church on Sunday, and, on Friday evening and Saturday evening, a mixture of persons to the two rival cinemas mentioned earlier. His mother had occasionally taken him and his brother on the picture bus, as it was called, to watch some or another comedy film at the Plaza or the Paramount. The bus had been always crowded – these were the years before television – and the pairs of passengers who had seemed to him boyfriends and girlfriends were dressed in what were almost certainly their best outfits and conducted themselves as though an evening at the Plaza or the Paramount was one of the chief events in their lives.

Only four years after Darlene had asked whether he was interested in films, he had begun writing in a journal long essays meant to decide how he could best express the wealth of meaning that he felt urged to express: whether the best means available to him was film or live theatre or prose fiction or poetry. The writer of the essays thought highly of film, but the young man, hardly more than a boy, who was asked about his interest in films thought at once not of a screen covered by images expressing a wealth of meaning but of the dark interior of the picture bus late on a Friday or a Saturday evening. The young persons in the bus, some of them no older than himself and the young woman who had questioned him, had seemed to expect much from film while they had travelled in the bus, a few hours earlier, towards the Plaza or the Paramount but had seemed on their journey homeward to have been disappointed. The young man who had been questioned and who had sometimes himself travelled with his mother in the picture bus could not have explained the disappointment of the young travellers homeward, but some or another man in the same wing of this building where I presently sit writing – some or another man may be about to write that the travellers homeward had earlier looked forward to seeing images of actual persons in actual places by definition more worthy of notice than the streets through which the picture bus travelled; the travellers had been able for a few hours to study the behaviour of their betters and to learn superior ways of dressing, of speaking, of kissing, even. Now, the travellers were back in the picture bus, and even if they turned away from one another and looked hopefully outwards they saw only vague images of themselves in an image-bus travelling through actual darkness.

In a work of fiction intended to provide its readers with the sort of experience available to watchers of film, a young male character might well be reported as seeing in his mind image after image of himself and a young female character while he and she travelled in the picture bus from their suburb to a neighbouring suburb, while they sat together in the Plaza or the Paramount, and while they later travelled homeward in the bus. The images would have appeared to the young male character soon after he had been asked by the young female whether he was interested in pictures; by which she meant sequences of images shown in places such as the Plaza or the Paramount. The same images would have appeared again to the young male character on the afternoon after he had been questioned and while he was walking with deliberate slowness through the streets of the inner suburb where he attended school so that he would arrive at the railway station after his usual train had left.

He recalls little. He may even have travelled with Darlene on a few more afternoons and talked with her as before, but within a few days he was travelling home alone on a later train. He had simply withdrawn; he had fled; he had run away from her. He doubts whether he felt any shame. For many years afterwards, he could not conceive of any different course available to him, given the sort of person he was at the time. He went on living in the same suburb for four more years. He travelled often by train and shopped often in the adjoining suburb and even went occasionally with his mother or his brother to the Plaza or the Paramount but he always remembered to look out for her in the distance. Sometimes he saw her from far off and loitered or changed direction. If they had suddenly come face to face, he would have dropped his eyes and hurried by.

One of the daily newspapers at that time included a weekly column offering advice to persons with problems, mostly of the sort that might have been called romantic. He read the column sometimes. The persons with problems used pen-names such as 'Puzzled' or 'Confused' or 'Heart-broken' and no detail of their addresses was ever published, not even the name of their suburb or town, so that he thought of them as belonging to an adult society almost as remote as that depicted in films. At some time during the first months after he had ceased to travel with Darlene, he had read the following answer to a questioner. (Not even the actual questions were published – only the columnist's answers.) 'What a churlish fellow! Seemingly he did not wish to continue the friendship but lacked the moral courage to say so. Forget about him. You are well rid of him.'

If ever he had asked himself, during all the years since, how a person might feel on seeming to recognise as a version of himself or herself some or another personage in a work of fiction, then he ought to have tried to recall whatever he had felt on learning that a wise and eloquent female person in a tall city building, seated at a desk covered with letters from hundreds of puzzled or confused young female persons, had read a report of certain behaviour of his, and had declared in writing to her many thousands of readers that he was a moral coward who deserved to be forgotten by the young woman who had exchanged glances with him for two years. Sometimes, in later years, he supposed that his having read the answer quoted ought to have shamed and humiliated him; that he ought to have felt as though he had been dragged by uniformed female attendants to the desk of the columnist herself who, dressed in the costume of the Queen Bee or the Empress of the Amazons, had shrieked to his face that he lacked moral courage. He suspects, however, that his main concern was that Darlene had not understood his motives for ending their friendship, as she must have described it.

He must also have been affected by the fact of Darlene's having written about him. On some or another evening, she had sat with pen and paper and had focused her thoughts on some or another image of him. He must have been thus affected, because the only other details that he recalls from that time are phrases from a letter that he found himself often composing in his mind: a letter that he might have sent to Darlene in order to explain his odd-seeming behaviour and perhaps even to suggest that he and she should become pen-friends for the time being. Perhaps he was dissuaded from writing the letter only by his not knowing Darlene's address. Few households in the outer suburbs had telephones at that time, and neither his nor Darlene's parents were listed in the directory. He knew the name of her street, but it was a long street and his only means of learning the number of her house might have been to follow her homeward at a distance as he had tried to follow homeward the first of his dark-haired girlfriends-in-the-mind. Any letter would have had to be sent in care of the columnist, the giver of advice, and she who had urged Darlene to forget him might have refused to pass his letter on.

Did he ever reflect on the folly of the columnist's telling Darlene to forget him? He was sure that she still remembered him, just as he still remembered her, although it was the silent Dathar that he mostly recalled rather than the talkative Darlene whose words, or almost all of them, had been seemingly lost on him. He never afterwards forgot the dark-haired young woman, hardly more than a girl, who had sat silently in sight of him on many an afternoon for almost two years. He never forgot that she had replied at once and in kind to the only written message he had sent her, although he had misread her reply. A certain version of him had even written, twenty years later, certain pages of fiction about her, and the pages had later been published. If I were to learn that someone, perhaps in this very corridor, is writing still more about her, then it would seem to me as though a certain sort of man might feel compelled to send messages in writing to a certain sort of dark-haired young woman and, when she had not at first sent a message in return, might be compelled to send further messages at intervals of twenty or twice that many years.

Yesterday evening, when I looked along the corridor most likely to lead past the rooms where are conceived and written the fictional texts so often referred to in this present text, I brought to mind still another possible subject fit to be *treated* by the occupants there, to use a word much favoured by Henry James whenever he came to write about his way of writing.

He who would be best able to treat the possible subject, as I called it, would have spent the last three of his years at school in one or another second-storey classroom with a view of several suburbs in what would be called nowadays the inner south-east of the city where he had been born. The school stood at one end of a long broad valley at the lowest part of which a creek flowed. Whatever might have been the earnings and the bank balances of the families in the suburbs along the valley, he, the possible narrator of what I have in mind, never doubted that all of the families were incomparably better off than was his own family, who lived in a newly settled outer suburb far from the valley. Perhaps half of his classmates lived in the suburbs of the valley, and although many of them were sons of bank-tellers and shipping clerks and lesser public servants, he considered even those families much more fortunate than his own. The tuition fees of the school would be considered modest if converted into the currency of today, but he and his brother incurred no fees – their father had pleaded with the principal when they were first enrolled that he, the father, could not afford even a token fee. He who often looked out across the valley supposed he was the only charity-boy in his class, although he learned many years later that the religious brothers, his teachers, were forbidden by the constitution of their order to turn away any boy whose parents could not pay for his schooling. It would have been prudent of the brothers not to have this known, but he who thought himself the only charity-boy learned also long afterward that he was one of many.

The creek still flows along the floor of the valley, but a freeway, dense with motor-traffic, now occupies what was formerly open space nearby. Local councils had built many football ovals and cricket pitches and a few grandstands and toilet blocks on the land beside the creek. Elsewhere were grasslands or clumps of gorse or bulrushes – places mostly deserted except for a few persons walking dogs or flying model aeroplanes.

On every Wednesday afternoon of the school-year, the senior classes travelled by tram to one or another point low in the valley and then on foot along the creek to one or another oval, there to play football or cricket. He, the chief character of this possible narrative, preferred open grassy places to streets lined with houses but he was seldom at ease beside the creek. He was pleased to stand comparatively alone while fielding at deep mid-on during a cricket match or while he was full-forward for his football team and play was at the other end – he could feel the wind in his face or could hear the goldfinches twittering above the gorse-bushes or even, after the spring rains, the creek rushing between jumbled rocks, but always he could see in the distance the streets after streets of houses where lived the residents of the valley, his supposed betters. From many a sportsground he could see not merely a blur of tiled roofs and green treetops but the details of some or another house, often of two storeys, that was the last house in some or another quiet dead-end street leading from a tree-lined avenue higher up towards the flood-plain of the creek. He who shared with his brother a cramped fibro-cement bungalow in a backyard and who did his homework at a kitchen table could hardly visualise the circumstances of some or another young man, hardly more than a boy, who studied each evening in a room that he alone occupied, at his own desk, and with his own bookshelf nearby and through the window above his desk a view of whole suburbs on the far side of a valley where many a house was of more than one storey and where many an upper window would appear strangely golden when lit by sunlight in the late afternoon.

He who struggled to visualise the details reported in the previous sentence had another reason for feeling uncomfortable beside the creek that flowed through the valley that he saw on most days in the distance. The sportsfields were so far from his school that he was seldom able on a Wednesday to catch the train that carried in the rear compartment of its front carriage a certain dark-haired young woman, hardly more than a girl, mentioned elsewhere in this work of fiction. He travelled homewards in a later train, hoping the young woman understood that Wednesday was sports day at his school and might even have divined that while she was travelling homeward as usual he was detained in what he considered enemy territory: in suburbs where young persons of both genders disdained to approach one another respectfully and warily but met boldly at tennis clubs during weekends or telephoned one another during evenings, looking out, while they talked, across the same valley and each trying to see the other's window in the distance.

The events reported in the following paragraphs on account of their being perhaps suitable for fictional treatment, to use that word once more – those events are to be understood as having taken place several months after the young man mentioned in the previous paragraphs had supposed that he was the subject of a paragraph in a newspaper column in which the female columnist accused an unidentified young man of moral cowardice.

On a certain cold and cloudy afternoon, the chief participant in the treatable events had played with nearly forty of his own age and gender a football match on an oval in a remote part of the valley mentioned earlier. The oval where the match had been played had no changing-rooms or toilet-block, and all those who had played were obliged to change clothes in among the many clumps of gorse along the creek. Many had already changed and were setting out across the parklands towards the nearest tram-stop when he, the chief participant, heard a young man close by calling out that he had found something strange. Only a few young men went to investigate, the rest being probably anxious to set out homeward. What had been found, in long grass under a gorse-bush, was an elegant-looking leather case with the initials of the owner stamped in gold on the upper side. The case contained textbooks and exercise-books belonging to a young man who would have been hardly more than a boy, given that he was in the same form or level as were the finders of the case. The owner of the books attended a boys' grammar school that would have been called by journalists of the time the most exclusive school of its kind in the capital city. The father of the owner, as the finders learned from the letterhead on a page of note-paper in an unsealed envelope in the case, was a specialist dentist with a suite of rooms in the street of the capital city where whole buildings were occupied at that time by specialist medical practitioners and dentists. The owner, as the finders learned from a handwritten note signed by the father, had been absent from school for several weeks past after having contracted chicken-pox. Even if the case had not contained, in addition to the book and the note, a cap and a necktie in the colours of the exclusive school, so to call it, the finders would soon have understood why the case had been lying under a gorse-bush by the creek. The owner of the case had done what any of the finders would have done if he had had such an opportunity as the owner had had. They would have played truant, as their fathers or teachers might have said, or, in their own words, they would have played the wag or wagged it. They would have hidden their schoolbooks and theirs caps and ties and would have spent the day in the city, playing pinball or lolling in a cinema.

Even those among the finders who themselves lived in the suburbs of the valley – even those seemed eager to embarrass or humiliate the son of the specialist dentist: the boy no older than themselves who would have spent the day in the city while his father thought him at school and while his teachers and schoolmates thought him at home and ill. The original finder of the case used a red pencil to add to the father's note a postscript advising that his son intended to wag school on the day after the note had been written. Someone else tore out a clean double-page from an exercise book and scrawled a rhyming couplet that he seemed to have composed for the occasion: *If a boy plays the wag from school / he should be strung up by the tool.* Others could think only of defacing pages of exercise books and textbooks with messages such as *Get fucked, grammar-school cunt!* When the finders had tired of their fun, they closed the case, with their messages uppermost among the contents, and replaced it in the long grass where its owner had hidden it.

The chief participant, as I called him earlier, had stood back and had watched all that is reported in the previous paragraphs – not because he had no wish to make trouble for the son of the specialist dentist but because he was reduced to inaction by his very eagerness to do so. While his schoolmates were tearing out pages and scrawling messages, he was struggling to comprehend his sudden good fortune. He had previously been able only to visualise certain young men of his own age, hardly more than boys, as mere presences behind upper-storey windows on the far side of their valley and to feel towards them only a generalised envy and resentment. Now, he had one of them in his power. He, the chief participant, knew the name of his enemy and his address, which was written on the lining of the cover of the leather case. He, the chief participant, had only to consult a street directory in order to learn where exactly his enemy's house stood in relation to the creek and the sportsfield. Given that the truant had hidden his case where he had, the house must have been close by. On every Wednesday afternoon in future he, the chief participant, might well be able to see from the sportsfield the very house, surely of two storeys and perhaps even with attic or dormer windows, where the specialist dentist lived with his family and even, in the shortest days of winter, the very window of his enemy's room picked out by the sunlight of late afternoon.

He, the chief participant, stood back and watched and tried to comprehend and soon found himself composing the text of a message that he might well have written on some or another blank page as soon as his schoolmates had done with their defacing the contents of the leather case. He was still standing and composing when the finder of the case closed down the lid and replaced the case in the long grass where he had found it. He, the chief participant, was still composing the opening sentences of the message while he walked towards the nearest tram stop and later while he travelled by train towards his outer suburb, sometimes recalling, perhaps, that he, or someone closely resembling himself, had been described in a column of a widely read newspaper as a moral coward because he could not have begun to explain to a certain young woman, hardly more than a girl, why he did not want to sit beside her in a cinema in the suburb adjoining their own. He, the chief participant, composed further sentences of the message from time to time during the fifty and more years following the cold and cloudy afternoon when his schoolmate had found the leather case under the gorse-bush. If challenged to do so, he could compose further sentences of the message in the house of two or, perhaps, three storeys where, presumably, he is preparing to turn into his preferred sort of fiction some at least of the substance, so to call it, of the paragraphs hereabouts.

The contents and the tenor of his message have been much altered during the past fifty and more years. He who merely watched while his schoolmates scrawled their simple messages – he could not have denied that he resented the dentist's son's having for his own use an upper-storey room overlooking a valley, a well-stocked set of bookshelves, and whatever else was provided for him from his father's substantial income, but his, the watcher's, chief difference with his enemy, as he considered him, concerned his ways with young women, hardly more than girls. He who merely watched would never have conceded that his own ways were open to question, but he recognised that many another a young man, hardly more than a boy, employed far other ways, at first sight much less demanding and less arduous than his own. He whose way was first to observe and then to begin to speculate about some or another young woman, hardly more than a girl and preferably dark-haired, and then to begin to compose the first of many written messages needing to be sent to her before he could prepare to approach her – he who would much rather have read in solitude a frank and eloquent letter from a person known to him as Dathar than have sat in a cinema beside a person known to him as Darlene was well aware that many a son of a specialist dentist, or even of a bank-teller or a shipping-clerk, was able to play tennis on many a weekend with many a young woman, hardly more than a girl, and afterwards to sit with her and to sip soft drinks and to talk with her while she was still wearing her short tennis-skirt or was able even to go with one of the young women to a cinema on many a Saturday evening and afterwards to escort her to her front door. He whose way was to compose messages or to wish to read messages was aware also that the young men mentioned in the previous sentence would mostly have been satisfied with their way of treating with the young women mentioned there whereas the composer of messages was sometimes made weary by his having to compose messages. And so, the message that he composed in earlier years, while it was intended to deride, was partly driven by envy. In later years, the message became more of a commentary. The composer of the message had come to accept that the man he addressed was never likely to read the message, perhaps not even in the unlikely event that the message had been finally written and then delivered to him. The commentary, so to call it, merely reported the differing ways of two sorts of man, neither of whom could have changed his ways, even if he had sometimes wanted to do so. By the time when the composer of the message had found his way into this building and into the very corridor where this account of him is being written, the tenor, as I called it earlier – the tenor of his composition had so changed that the composer of messages seemed almost to be commiserating with a man who might have had by then several wives and numerous sexual partners and who might have watched hundreds of films in dozens of cinemas while his commiserator had been composing message after message for the dark-haired personage that he was yet to meet up with.

During the years when I used to read the reviews of works of fiction published in newspaper supplements or in so-called literary magazines, one of the words that I most often puzzled over was the word *character*. Writers of fiction, so I often read, *created characters*, some of whom were *believable* while others were not so. One or another reviewer might admit to *caring about* the characters said to be *in* a certain work of fiction while another reviewer might gainsay a certain work because he or she was *unable to care* for the characters said to be *in* the work. Sometimes a writer of fiction would be praised because he or she had adequately explained the motivation of his or her characters: the reasons for their having behaved as they had. Or, a writer might be blamed for failing to account for the behaviour of his or her characters. I would surely have read many a review in which characters and their motives were never mentioned, but I recall no reviewer or critic who insisted that fictional characters ought not to be discussed as though they are persons living in the world where books of fiction are written and read. In this connection, however, I can report that I once read with approval a statement by the writer of fiction Evelyn Waugh. He had never, Waugh wrote, entertained the least interest in *why* his characters behaved as they did. Waugh may have belonged among the great number who seem to think of fictional characters rather as they think of actual persons, but at least he felt no obligation to try to read the minds of his creatures, so to call them.

While I was writing the previous paragraph, I remembered an illustration that I saw as a child on the cover of some or another history textbook. The illustration was of a book resting vertically with its spine rearward, its covers parted so as to form almost a right angle, and many of its pages standing slightly apart. In the foreground appeared the nearest of a throng of crowned kings and queens, knights in armour, and persons in robes or tunics or animal skins. Behind these, in the middle ground, more such figures were advancing from between the pages of the book while further off, in the background, were rudimentary figures or mere blurs only partly detached as yet from the lines of text that had given rise to them and to all those ahead of them. A child might have supposed, from the faces and the bearing of the foremost figures, that they were pleased and relieved to have fulfilled at last their true destiny: to have escaped from the confines of printed pages and to have arrived in the actual, visible world where they could shed their former mysteriousness and could deal as equals with those who were previously able only to read about them.

I have sometimes tried to explain what I consider a widespread confusion about the nature of what I call fictional personages. I have sometimes supposed that too many readers – and writers also – expect the reading of fiction to yield the sort of experience seemingly provided by the watching of films. I have sometimes

supposed that those same readers and writers have been too
much influenced by certain theories devised during the twentieth
century to explain the workings of the mind. But these are mere
suppositions, and they seem doubtful indeed when I recall what
little I can recall from my having read long ago some of the
fiction by Charles Dickens or George Eliot or William Thackeray,
who were writing long before the development of the cinema or
the dissemination of the theories of Sigmund Freud. (Am I right
to have omitted Emily Brontë from the few that I named just now
and to take satisfaction from my never having watched any of the
several films titled *Wuthering Heights* or from my never having
understood why any of the characters, so to call them, in the book
of the same name behaved as they are reported to have behaved?)

I was probably foolish to have tried just now to account for
beliefs and expectations so different from my own. I am surely
entitled to do no more than to report my informed speculations
as to what happens sometimes in this corridor, in those rooms
where a certain sort of fictional personage might be said to come
into being.

The next section of this work of fiction will comprise a report
of the dealings, during a period of no less than sixty years,
between a certain occupant of this corridor and a certain fictional
personage, so to call her. What follows here is a summary of many
drunken debates in the common room of this wing and almost as
many sober discussions on far-reaching pathways in the grounds
around, or on shaded seats by sequences of trickling pools in
secluded ferneries. The sort of writer most likely to find his way

to the corridors hereabouts and to consider our ways congenial – that sort of writer has seldom tried to fit into any system the jumble of beliefs and suppositions and presentiments and instinctive preferences acquired during a lifetime, but we are able to agree on some matters. Most of us agree, for example, that we were too timid as young writers and too respectful of custom, so that our earlier works of fiction include reports of deeds done or words said or daydreams entertained by entities likely to be taken for characters by most readers. The most eloquent of this majority, although we share many of his beliefs, nevertheless wearies even us with his constant railing, as I may be about to weary the reader with my report of it. He, the eloquent one, can never begin a discussion about what he calls the ghosts above the pages without first belittling those readers or commentators who speak or write about Tess Durbeyfield or Catherine Earnshaw or Maggie Verver or others of their kind as though they are beings hardly different from you, whatever sort of reader you may be, or from me, the writer of these words, or from our next-door neighbours or the persons who served us yesterday in our local shops: persons of flesh and blood who breathe, digest food, sweat, and break wind. He professes to despise those who read fiction for no better purpose than to learn what they might more easily learn by listening to their neighbours' quarrels or by getting drunk with their workmates. A so-called character from fiction, he says, struggling, so I always suppose, with terms that have no meaning for him – a so-called character belongs by definition in the invisible world, and no dweller in that world is perceptible to more than one dweller in this, the visible world. The eloquent one, as I called him, has told us more than once that a certain now-famous writer of fiction, at his desk in an upstairs room on the far side of the globe, would once have had in mind a certain image-personage. Nearly a hundred years later, he, the eloquent one, had happened to read certain sentences the import of which seemed to be that a certain young woman, hardly more than a girl, and bearing the name Tess Durbeyfield, might be supposed to have lived, at some or another time now passed, at some or another site in some or another visible world...He has told this to us often but has always broken off at the same point in his argument, as if he demeaned himself by explaining what was surely obvious to the dullest reader of fiction.

He calls them, this occasionally drunken and voluble but mostly sober and taciturn man – he calls them sometimes, as I wrote earlier, ghosts above the pages or, sometimes, casters of fictional shadows. He has said more than once that these presences, which is another of his names for them, are to him what their deities and saints are to the followers of religions. He speaks often as though, from some ultimate vantage-point, his ghosts or presences might prove to be the actual and we who try to write or to read about them the shadowy. I recall my asking him one evening, when the common-room was suddenly in gloom after the last shafts of sunlight had passed from the nearby panes – I recall my asking him how he could dare to seem to limit or to diminish the beings he so venerated by writing fiction in which semblances of them could be said to be recognisable. He evaded my question but gave me an answer that silenced me, even so. He asked me to recall some or another recent dream of mine in which some or another dream-character or dream-personage had behaved contrary to my wishes or my expectations. I was able at once to recall such a dream and such an instance as he had described. Then, while I was still in somewhat the same mood of confusion and disappointment that would have overcome me when I awoke from the dream itself, he declared that he or she who had angered me or had disappointed me or had consoled me bore the same relationship to the agent truly responsible for my mood as a so-called character in a work of fiction bears to the personage who seems to stand beside the writer while he or she writes or beside the reader while he or she reads.

During all the time while I was writing the previous six paragraphs, some or another image has appeared to me from among the sequences of images that would first have appeared to me twenty-five years ago, while I was reading for the first time a piece of short fiction sent as an unsolicited contribution to a periodical that employed me for several years to help select fiction for publication. Before I had finished even my first reading of the piece, I had decided to recommend it for publication, and it was later published. Of all the other pieces that I would have thus recommended I recall only a few titles, a few authors' names, and a few imprecise images that would have occurred to me while I read the pieces, which I usually read only once. In connection with the piece of fiction mentioned just now, I cannot claim to recall what happened during my first reading for the reason that I have been drawn to read the piece a number of times during the twenty-five years since, so that the images brought to my mind and the feelings linked to the images have been often augmented or renewed and I am often able to recall whole sentences from the text itself. The title of the piece is 'The Characters of Nineteenth-Century Fiction', and the author is Louise Davenport. The text, which comprises fewer than a thousand words, begins with the sentence 'She wanted to squash the characters she read about in nineteenth-century fiction.' The remainder of the text reports that the chief character kept many of the characters of nineteenth-century fiction in matchboxes; that on a certain day she killed the characters one after another in her parents' bedroom – not by squashing them but by breaking their tiny bodies with a toy axe; that she then took the matchboxes full of the dead, broken bodies of the fictional persons out into the sunshine and carried them to a shallow irrigation channel on the boundary of her parents' property in the north-central district of the state where I sit writing these words; that she waded into the channel and emptied the matchboxes into the muddy water among clumps of bulrushes; and that she afterwards returned home and began to rake the grass-cuttings left by her brother, who was mowing their parents' lawn.

Her name is Torfrida, and he has never during the past fifty years thought of her as any sort of character from any sort of fiction, he being the occupant of some or another room not far from this room. (If the doors after doors along the dim corridors hereabouts had nameplates or even numerals on them, I could be more precise, but when once I tried to suggest such a system I was told, somewhat pompously, it seemed to me, that bright lighting and unambiguous labelling would be not at all in keeping with the tasks undertaken in this part of the building, which tasks have always been agreed to possess a certain mysteriousness, or so I was told.) He claims that no word in the language denotes the class of being that she belongs to. Sometimes, for the sake of convenience, he calls her a ghost, but he ought rather, he tells us, to use the odd-sounding term *haunter*, given that the verb *to haunt* comes close to defining her dealings with him. While he admits that certain passages in a certain work of fiction were in some way connected with his becoming aware of her, if he were to set about making notes – here, in this very corridor and on this very afternoon – for a fictional account of her connection with him, he would surely begin by mentioning not only a certain book but certain places, a certain piece of music, and even a certain weather, as though to allow for the possibility that she might have appeared to him, so to speak, at a certain time and in a certain place no matter what fictional text happened to be in his hands.

He was mostly deprived of books during his schooldays. The few books in his parents' house were of little interest to him. No school that he attended was equipped with a library. Even his secondary school, in a suburb that would have been called middle-class, had not even a shelf of books in any classroom. In his fifteenth year, he learned that a circulating library for young persons had been recently established in an upstairs room in the shopping centre near his school. When he registered himself as a borrower, he was made uneasy by several prominent signboards announcing that the library was a project of the ladies' committee of the local branch of the Liberal Party. He understood that his parents voted for the Labor Party, as had *their* parents, and regarded the Liberals as the party of the oppressors, and so he felt obliged to tell his father who it was who had made available the books that he, the borrower, had begun to bring home. His father was at once suspicious and for some weeks inspected every book but decided in time that they were harmless. Even he, the borrower, was at first wary of the mostly white-haired women who registered his borrowings and returnings and was relieved that they did not preach to him on political topics.

The library was quite unlike any of the places that go by that name nowadays. It occupied a large room above a shop in a street of shops. The only items of furniture were the table where the white-haired women sat and the shelves around the walls where books were stored. There was nowhere any sort of poster or what might be called nowadays a promotional display. He, the chief character of these paragraphs, could not recall in later years having seen any picture books or non-fiction books in the library, although this may be due to his having been interested only in the collection of fiction. This comprised many hundreds of titles, all with cloth covers and all second-hand. Despite his feeling in great need of books, he mostly struggled to find a volume of interest to him. He believes nowadays that he visited the library for only a few months before deciding that he had read every book with a claim on him. He recalls having read every volume he could find with Robert Louis Stevenson as its author and still recalls a few of his experiences as a reader of them. He recalls likewise several books by Charles Dickens. He recalls the fact of his having read *Lorna Doone*, by an author whose name he long ago forgot, but of his experience as a reader of the book he recalls nothing, although he seems to recall, from the few hours after he had borrowed the book but before he had begun to read it, his looking forward to reading about the setting, so to call it, of the narrative, which setting, or so he believed, was remote moorland. Finally, he recalls his having read a number of books by an author whose name appeared on the books as *D.K. Broster* and who may have been a woman, or so he was told by someone many years afterwards. From the many hours that he must have spent in reading those books, all of which he believes to have been of the kind often called historical fiction, he recalls only a few moments that he has sometimes recalled during the sixty years since those moments passed. He seems to recall that he was reading at the time a book with the title *The Flight of the Heron*. He certainly recalls that the historical setting, so to call it, of the book in question was the Vendean War, so to call it, which took place in the south-west of France during the first years after the Revolution. He recalls that the chief character of the book was a young man, probably an aristocrat and certainly a devout Roman

Catholic, as were most of the rebels taking part in the so-called war. He, the man recalling, felt little sympathy that he can recall for the chief character, who seemed to him too virtuous and proper. And yet, after sixty years during which he forgot all else that he may have experienced while reading several books by D.K. Broster, he still recalls his reading, towards the end of the book, a report of the chief character's learning from a letter, and at a time when the Vendean forces were hard pressed, that the young woman with whom he had been for long in love and with whom he had had, or so he supposed, an understanding – the young woman had married or had betrothed herself to another man. From one or another of the pages of text towards the end of the book, he, the man recalling, is able to recall an actual phrase. The third-person narrator, claiming to have access to the thoughts and feelings of the chief character, and using almost the very technique that I called earlier *double voicing*, reports that the young woman mentioned had for long been to the young man *his guiding star*, or it may have been *his shining star*.

And yet, along with the few fragments that are all he has preserved from the many hours when he looked along shelf after shelf in the drab upper room, first taking down and then looking into and then mostly replacing the one after another of the books in their dull-coloured cloth-and-boards, from the many hours when he sat or stood in some or another railway carriage, staring at the opened pages in front of him or glancing, whenever he turned a page, at some or another young woman, hardly more than a girl, who sat or stood nearby but always looking back at the pages before she returned his glance, and from the many hours of an evening after he had washed or dried the tea dishes with his brother and had done his homework at the wooden kitchen table with linoleum glued to its top and had sat until his bedtime at the same table with his library book open in front of him – along with those few fragments, he has been aware during the past sixty years of a certain personage, so to call her, who first appeared to him while he was reading a certain book of fiction borrowed from the upper room: a personage worthy to be called, if he were to use the language of false poetry such as was used by D.K. Broster, his own guiding star or shining star.

I would be misleading the reader if I were to report that Torfrida is a character in a work of fiction with the title *Hereward the Wake* by Charles Kingsley. I am able to state as a fact that he who deals, of course, not in facts but in fictional truths once read the book of that name, which book, so he seems to recall, even contained a duotone reproduction of a portrait of a fair-haired female person, which portrait was intended, surely, to suggest to the reader what would have been the appearance of a female character, so to call her, mentioned often in the adjacent pages of text if that character had been an actual person. But I am able to state as well that the personage known to him during the past sixty years as Torfrida appears to him as a young woman, hardly more than a girl, with dark hair and lacking altogether the fictional history of the fictional character in the work of fiction by Charles Kingsley.

What does he, researcher among works of fiction never

published or never even projected – what does he recall from his having read the work of fiction *Hereward the Wake*? He recalls that Hereward the Wake is the leader of a band of English rebelling against the Normans soon after their conquest of England; that the stronghold of the rebels is in the fen districts; that Hereward marries Torfrida when both are young but that he later has another woman as his consort, after he and Torfrida have separated. He, the researcher, as I call him, believes he recalls also that Torfrida has her first sight of Hereward when she looks down at him from the window of an upper room. Of all that must have passed through his mind during the many hours while he read the hundreds of pages between the maroon-coloured covers of the bulky borrowed book, he recalls nothing more. And yet, at some time while he read, he became acquainted, as it were, with the image of a dark-haired female ghost-above-the-pages who was to haunt him during the remainder of his life, to use the terms most favoured by the writer mentioned in the previous section of this work of fiction.

He would find it difficult to include Torfrida as even a ghostly character in any sort of fictional writing. She came to him without any seeming history, although her mere presence is powerful enough to suggest to him numerous possibilities in both her past and her future. Rather than struggling to write about her, he is mostly content to accept her existence as incontrovertible proof that the reading and the writing of fiction are much more than a mere transaction during which one person causes another person to see in mind a sort of shadowy film; that the whole enterprise of fiction exists mostly to enable her and numerous others of her kind to flit from place to place in mind after mind as though many a fictional text is a mere bridge or stairway raised for their convenience of travel.

No one in this wing owns to being a poet. Several may have written one or more poems, but whether or not any such occasional poet has sought publication, no published poem can be traced back to these dusty corridors and mostly silent rooms. Poets we may not claim to be, but some of us will sometimes discuss at length the differences or the likenesses between sentences and verses or between paragraphs and stanzas; what purpose, if any, is served by the use of metaphors; whether or not a sentence can be said to have a rhythm even though it lacks for metre; and many other such matters. We discuss these things freely even though none of us calls himself a poet, and we find it curious that these topics are of interest to us but are never raised in a certain corridor in the wing adjoining ours. Some of us lunch or dine or carouse sometimes in that corridor, although few of us feel at home there. Among ourselves, we call the occupants of that corridor the renegade poets. They were young men when to be young and to be declaiming poems in public places was to feel oneself at the bubbling centre of a spring that would soon become a torrent and would cleanse the world, as one or another of them might have written at the time. But soon, a change occurred in the upper atmosphere where the winds of fashion arise, and those winds began to blow in a different direction, to put the matter poetically again, and many who had looked forward to changing the world found this particular change hard to bear, this passing of the craze for poetry, and so they took to writing novels, as they called their newest works, many of which might have passed for scripts of documentary films, with themselves and their disorderly lives for subject-matter. Those of us who consort sometimes with the renegades long ago gave up asking them to explain their changing from fashionable poets to equally fashionable novelists. The renegades seem to have learned long ago the advantages of evasiveness or, perhaps, of using expressions such as *beautifully written* or *moving* or *powerful* in order to hide their ignorance of the craft of fiction. Most of us believe them to have written their pretend-filmscripts from the same motive that drove them three and more decades ago, to declaim their poetic protests: from a wish to be entitled to swagger, especially in the presence of female persons. And some of us, when drunk, have even put to the renegades, as though in jest, what most of us long ago decided, namely that their turning from poetry to prose was of hardly any moment, given that what they had called poetry was no more than badly punctuated prose arranged in lines of arbitrary length.

We happen to have among us one who freely admits to being a failed poet, although he reminds us often that he had taken up and had later abandoned poetry before the decades when the renegades were most prolific. As a very young man, so he once told us, he had believed in metaphor as some persons believe in religious creeds or political manifestos. He had even hoped to get from the contemplation of metaphor what some so-called mystics are said to get from their contemplation of the divine or the ultimate. Unlike the renegades, our failed poet is by no means evasive when asked why he turned from poetry to prose, but when he sets out to explain his apostasy or conversion he uses an odd-seeming comparison. He likens poetry to whisky or gin and prose to beer, which is his only drink. He says the amount of alcohol in a given volume of beer constitutes a sort of perfect proportion or golden mean whereas whisky and other spirits are akin to poisons, with a potency out of all proportion to their volume. Poets, he says, are distillers while we writers of prose are brewers, and he strives while he writes to turn out sentence after sentence the meaning of which will keep his reader in a heightened state of awareness for hour after hour whereas the poet that he had once wanted to be might have had *his* reader fall forward, before long, to the table, seeing double after a surfeit of metaphors.

Our turncoat, as we sometimes call him in jest, counts among the unwritten pieces that he may yet write as supplements to his few brief published works a fictional account of certain events from his twenty-second year, one of them being his meeting up with a certain dark-haired young woman who, if ever he had tried to compare and to quantify the differing looks and features of all the dark-haired girls and young women he had taken note of, would have been one of the first among them. At the time of their meeting, he was a teacher in a primary school in an inner suburb of the city where he had been born. He worked conscientiously as a teacher but he was planning to resign at the end of the year, when his contract would have expired. He intended to work afterwards at menial jobs that would cause him none of the nervous stress, as he called it, that his teaching caused and would allow him to spend much of his free time writing poetry. He had no girlfriend at the time. He had had a girlfriend for a few months several years before, but he had bored her with his talk of books and poetry and he resented her wanting to go to dances or to cinemas. He felt much in need of a girlfriend but he could never have approached any of the young female teachers at his school, who talked in the staffroom mostly about television programs. He looked forward to acquiring a girlfriend from among the young female poets who would attend one of the literary gatherings that took place, so he had heard, at the time of publication of each number of the quarterly magazine to which he sent most of his poems. All of his poems had been politely returned to him by the editor of the magazine, but in the margin of one of the poems the editor had written a favourable comment. He, the young poet, expected soon to have one or more of his poems published and to meet at the literary gathering soon afterwards a female equivalent of himself and to begin with her the discussion and the exchanges of letters that would lead to their becoming boyfriend and girlfriend.

On a certain day towards the end of what our turncoat, so to call him, intended to be his last year as a teacher, the principal of his school brought to the door of his classroom the dark-haired young woman mentioned previously, introduced him to her, and told him that the young woman was an expert in the teaching of drama and would spend a half-hour in his classroom during each of the next four weeks teaching dramatic skills to his pupils.

Long afterwards, the teacher and poet came to understand the circumstances behind the unexpected appearance at his classroom door of the most noteworthy of all the dark-haired female persons he had met up with or had observed from a distance or whose images he had kept in mind. She had arrived from England not long before. She was entitled to put after her name a series of letters that intimidated the teacher-poet when he saw them during her first session in his classroom but which failed to intimidate the director of primary education after the young woman had gained an interview with him soon after her arrival from London, where she had completed the courses that had entitled her to put the series of letters after her name. She probably expected the director of primary education to appoint her at once to the staff of one or another training college for teachers as an expert in drama, but he allowed her only to visit one or another primary classroom each week for four weeks, to have charge of the children there for a half-hour each week, and then, during the fourth week, to demonstrate to the local district inspector of schools her skills as a teacher of drama. The school selected for her trial was the school where the young unpublished poet taught a fifth grade. He supposed, long afterwards, that the principal of the school would have approached several or, perhaps, all of his fellow teachers but that these would have refused to allow into their classrooms the pushy young Englishwoman with the fancy letters after her name, as they would have called her. He, the young teacher of a fifth grade, would not have thought of refusing the young woman, even if she had not seemed to him at once the most fetching of all the dark-haired female persons that he had admired or had kept in mind. He was not opposed to having visiting teachers lighten his own teaching duties. As well, he was at that time still far from developing the antipathy that he later developed towards live theatre, so to call it. He even supposed sometimes that he might compose, after he had established his reputation as a poet, such a poem as could be performed on stage as a poetic monologue, which was a phrase that he liked to hear in his mind.

He remembers nothing of what she taught, or tried to teach, to his pupils. He learned, some years afterwards and by chance, that she had later been on the staff of a teachers' training college, although he could not know whether this was a direct result of her dealings with his class. He remembers nothing of her final session in his class, when the district inspector of schools would have been present to assess her. (He suspects that he might have spent the time in the staffroom rather than watch her ordeal.) He remembers that she thanked him often and profusely for his help. When she left his class on each of her first three visits, she asked if he would rehearse with his pupils during the coming week some or another routine. This he did faithfully, as he would have done for any visiting teacher, and she always seemed overly grateful afterwards. They addressed each other always as *Mr* and *Miss*, which was not unusual for that time and that situation, and the nearest that either of them came to familiarity was her calling him a brick when they said goodbye after her last visit.

Not once did he think of her as a possible girlfriend. He supposed that she must have been a year or two older than he in order to have acquired so many letters after her name. That alone would have excused him from thinking of her romantically, as another sort of writer might have written. But even if he had wanted to meet with her during a weekend or an evening, he could only have foreseen the two of them sitting in a coffee-lounge or a cinema and himself feeling out of place or even wretched. He spent most of his free time at his desk in the rented room where he lived or in the Reading Room of the State Library. On several weekday evenings he drank beer, mostly alone, in a shabby hotel in the city, in a back bar frequented by people he considered bohemians. His solitary reading and writing and drinking seemed to him not so much a hardship as a sort of apprenticeship leading at last to his becoming a published poet and somewhat the equal of female persons with dark hair and memorable faces and many letters after their names.

Given what is reported in the previous paragraph, I need hardly report in this paragraph that he felt no more that a mild annoyance a few hours after her last visit when he found among the books and papers on his classroom table an envelope with her name typed on the front. She had sometimes spread pages of notes on his table, and he assumed that the envelope had spilled out of her large bag during her last visit and had been later overlooked. His annoyance came from his having to try to return the envelope to her when all he knew was her name, but when he handled the envelope he found it to be unsealed, and when he had opened the envelope he found inside a single typed page with the letterhead of a famous jeweller whose shop was in a fashionable quarter of the city. At the upper left of the typed page was the name of the young woman, although the series of letters was missing, and below the name was her address, which was in a suburb near his own. Much of the page was occupied by a list of items of jewellery owned by the young woman together with the estimated value of each item for the purpose of its being insured. Below the list was the signature of the valuer of the items. After he had read the page with the letterhead of the famous jeweller, he was relieved that he would be able to return the misplaced letter to its owner simply by inserting it into a larger envelope and then posting both to the address of the young woman, together with a few words explaining the matter. He recalls these events clearly, even more than fifty years later, and if ever he were to include these events, or a version of them, in a piece of fiction, he would have the narrator of the fiction assure the reader that the chief character of the fiction entertained at the time no possibility that the young woman with dark hair and the many letters after her name had not genuinely misplaced the letter from the famous jeweller, although he supposed briefly that a young man very different from himself might have dared to suppose otherwise.

On most evenings, a few of us spend an hour or more in the common room that serves this corridor. The room itself is a dreary space, hardly better furnished than the so-called commercial room that was provided in some of the two-storey hotels in country towns long ago, when numerous commercial travellers or sales representatives drove in their station wagons on the roads of the state where are set, so to speak, many sections of this work of fiction and needed, of an evening, a table or a desk-top where they could do what they called their paper-work while they drank their beer. The only books on the few shelves are so-called reference books: dictionaries, atlases, and those books that pronounce on correct usage of words, correct spelling of difficult proper nouns, and the like. The remainder of the shelves contain hundreds of back numbers of a soft-covered monthly publication, *The Australian Journal*. The earliest numbers date from the early 1930s while the most recent are from the late 1950s, when the *Journal*, so to call it, ceased publication after its former readers had taken to watching television during all of their leisure time. The man who deposited this publication on our shelves is almost the only one of us who looks into the back numbers. He has told us often that the collection had been amassed by his parents. They had bought and read the *Journal* from the first year of their marriage. As soon as he had learned to read, he had looked into whatever number was lying about the house and had tried to make sense of the text. As he grew older, he fell into the habit of reading every one of the dozen and more pieces of short fiction or short stories, as they were called, in every issue. He is aware, so he has often told us, that most of us dismiss those pieces or stories as popular fiction of no deep meaning or lasting worth, but he claims to have learned from the pieces or stories what he calls the power of straightforward narrative.

This same man told some of us one evening in the common room that he still recalled, sixty and more years afterwards, certain series of narrated events from some of the earliest numbers he had read of *The Australian Journal*, by which he meant not only the scenes that had appeared in his mind while he first read but some of the words of the narrative. Even when he examined what remained to him of books that might be called works of literature, the last traces, as he called them, nearly always comprised a narrative, however brief. He gave as an example an autobiography that he had read nearly thirty years before and had not looked into since. The author had flourished, as the old expression used to have it, in the mid-twentieth century as a paleontologist at several universities in the USA. The man had had a humble and a troubled upbringing. There was much difficulty between him and his mother, which resulted in his leaving home when he was a young man, hardly more than a boy, and having to live as a hobo for some years during the early 1930s. During one of those years, he had been camped alone at evening on a hillside near a railway line. He had lit a campfire and was cooking a simple meal. He understood that a freight train would pass close to the campsite later in the evening, and he intended to jump aboard the train when it was slowed by the hill. When his meal was almost ready, a dog came up to him. The dog appeared to be starving, and the man gave it a portion of his meal. After he and the dog had eaten, the dog rested beside the man as though he and it were now master and faithful servant, and the man speculated that he might have been the first person ever to have fed the dog or to have treated it less than harshly. As the time approached for the arrival of the freight train, the man stood beside the railway line with his pack on his back, and the dog stood close behind him. The man understood that he could not take the dog with him. Not only could he not succeed in getting both himself and the dog aboard the freight train, but he could not live the life of a hobo with a dog to provide for. When he heard the train approaching, the man stood ready to jump aboard. The hill where he stood was well-known among hoboes as a place for jumping aboard, and the man expected some of the hoboes already on the train to have opened some of the doors of the freight vans for someone such as himself. The train slowed; the man saw an open door; the man ran beside the train; the man clambered aboard. As soon as he was securely aboard, the man looked for the dog. He saw it keeping pace with the train and looking up at him. The dog was able to keep pace with the train for as long as it climbed the low hill, but when the train passed the hill, the dog began to fall behind. The man lay in the doorway of the freight van and watched the dog falling further behind. The man later wrote in his autobiography that he had recalled often during the remainder of his life his sight of the dog while it tried to keep pace with the train. He had recalled in particular his sight of the nearer eye of the dog while it tried to keep pace. The eye had seemed to be turned sideways and upwards, or so he had thought, as though the dog had struggled, before it lost sight for ever of the only person who had fed it or had treated it less than harshly, to fix in mind an image of that person.

While the man had been telling us in the common room what is reported above, one among us was seen to stop his ears with his fingers. Most of us surely knew that the man with his fingers to his ears believed himself to be following the example of Henry James, who is mentioned surprisingly often in our part of this building, in not wanting to hear to its end an anecdote that might later provide him with matter for fiction, and I was not surprised when there began in the room one of those inconclusive discussions that some of us seem to enjoy. I heard little of what went forward in the bare, harshly lit room. I was recalling a morning when I was in my twenty-first year and was preparing to move out of my parents' home. There was much difficulty between me and my mother at the time. Every Sunday morning, I would leave the house as though to walk to our parish church but would call instead at a milk-bar and would sit for an hour at a table inside, sipping a malted milk and reading from the pages of the *Sporting Globe* the results of horse-races contested on the previous day in every state of the country before returning home as though I had been to church. On one such morning, which I remember as having been cold and overcast, I happened to look at two children in the front yard of one of the many newly built weatherboard houses in the outer suburb

where I then lived. The front yard had not yet been turned into
any sort of garden. Between the front porch and the front fence
were tussocks of grass, clods of earth, and puddles of rainwater.
I supposed that the young man and his wife who had recently
bought the house had as yet no money to pay for paths or
lawn-seed or garden-plants. The two children that I happened
to look at were a girl and a boy. The girl may have been six
or seven years of age; the boy was a little younger. They were
playing the game that many children have surely played: one of
the two was a pretend-horse and was steered by the other with a
string or a cord. I cannot even recall which child was horse and
which was driver. Nor can I recall any detail of the appearance
of the boy. I recall only the girl and only the sight of her face
when she looked towards me during the first moments after she
had become aware that I was passing her house and that I had
noticed her and her brother playing among the clods and the
tussocks and the puddles. I seemed to learn from her face that
she was kindly disposed towards me; that she might have trusted
me if ever she had been obliged to do so; that if our circumstances
had been vastly different she would have welcomed me into her
game. And while the men around me in the common-room went
on with their debate as to the worth of anecdotes, I supposed that
my eyes must have been turned sideways and downwards while
I had passed the front yard where the children were playing, as
though I had wanted to fix in mind an image of the first female-
person who might have invited me into her pretend-world.

The detail about to be reported has not only stayed in my mind since my first and only reading, nearly forty years ago, of the work of fiction *Epitaph of a Small Winner*, by Machado de Assis but is the only detail that I can recall from my having read the work. The first-person narrator pauses in his account of his life-story, so to call it, and reports that a butterfly had come into his room through an open window a few minutes before and had alighted on his desk and had seemed to look at him as though he might have been the god of the butterflies.

The detail about to be reported has stayed in my mind since my first and only reading, nearly sixty years ago, of the work of fiction *The Mayor of Casterbridge*, by Thomas Hardy. As part of his effort to describe, as it were, the peculiar characteristics of the fictional town of Casterbridge, the narrator of the novel, so to call it, claims that the town merges so comfortably into the countryside surrounding it that many a butterfly urged to travel from some or another grassy landscape north of the town to some or another more congenial landscape south of the town chooses not to follow some or another long, circuitous course around the margins of the town but rather to flit through the town itself: to pass over roads and between shops and houses as though these are only recent and temporary alterations to the long-standing arrangement of things; as though the countryside is permanent and the town merely temporary.

When I first drew up the plan of this work of fiction, I intended this, the nineteenth of the thirty-four sections, to comprise an argument in favour of reliable narrators as against unreliable or absent narrators. (Unreliable narrators are most often discoverable from internal evidence, so to call it: the texts for which they are seemingly responsible are found to be inconsistent or self-contradictory. Fictional texts lacking narrators include those presented as collections of letters or of documents or of reports by a number of different first-person voices, so to call them. Such texts offer no explanation as to how they could have come into being: as to how the letters or documents or confessions, so to call them, came to be arranged as they are.) The notes that I made at the time are so brief that I cannot now recall the details of my intended argument. Moreover, it occurred to me just now, while I was writing the passage in parentheses above, that no discerning reader should need to be convinced of what is surely self-evident. When I begin to recall the dreary effect on me of even the brief passages that I have sometimes read in certain texts before deciding to read no further, then I feel confident that the discerning reader about to begin a work of fiction expects the personage seemingly responsible for the existence of the text to be seemingly approachable by way of the text or seemingly revealed through the text and to seem to have written the text in order to impart what could never have been imparted by any other means than the writing of a fictional text. In short, I feel confident that the discerning reader would prefer to be in the seeming presence of a personage who could be trusted to have once noted the passing of a butterfly above a street in the south of England or the alighting of a butterfly on his desk in a suburb of Rio de Janeiro than to have in front of him or her a mere text the seeming work of no recognisable personage.

When I first drew up the plan for this work of fiction, I intended that the last paragraph of this section would expound the final, persuasive claims of the argument that I cannot now remember. I shall include here instead something that occurred to me while I was writing about the butterflies mentioned above. A frequently repeated anecdote tells of a Chinese sage who dreamed of being a butterfly and who, on waking, questioned whether he was, in fact, a man who had dreamed of a butterfly-existence or quite the reverse. A discerning reader who had dreamed, or had seemed to dream, such a dream or a seeming-dream would surely ask, on awakening, not merely what the Chinese sage is reported to have asked but whether the butterfly or the seeming-butterfly was actual or fictional and, if it was fictional, whether or not the narrator reporting its existence was seemingly reliable and to be trusted.

He was reported in an earlier section of this work of fiction as having experienced, or having seemed to experience, as a younger man several of what were called at the time nervous breakdowns and as having during one such experience consulted a medical specialist but as having merely endured the other experiences until they had passed or had seemed to pass. He did not merely remain passive during each of those other experiences but took thought constantly as to how he might bring an end to the experience. He often supposed that his best means for recovering, so to speak, would be to meet up with a certain sort of female person or to read a certain sort of work of fiction with a trustworthy narrator. Even while he was consulting the medical specialist, he still supposed that he was more likely to recover by one of the means mentioned just now than as a result of his taking the medicines or following the advice provided by the medical specialist. As time passed, however, without his having met the certain sort of female person or having read the certain sort of work of fiction, he drew on his memories of what he had read in certain books, some of them being works of fiction with narrators not necessarily trustworthy, and began to conduct himself in the company of the medical specialist as though he, the nervously broken one, was a character in a work of fiction with a narrator not necessarily trustworthy. (The medical specialist, from the time of their first meeting, had been conducting himself thus.)

This and the following few paragraphs will be more easily written and more easily read if I report of the chief character that he *pretended* to do this or that rather than that he did this or that as though he was a character in a work of fiction with a narrator not necessarily trustworthy. He had satisfied himself, during his first visits to the medical specialist, that the man subscribed to certain popular theories as to what constitutes the mind and what are the causes of mental disorders and the most effective treatments of them. After he, the broken-down one, had begun to pretend, he pretended first that he too subscribed to the theories mentioned just now, then that his having broken down, almost certainly not for the first time, was a result of difficulties that had for long existed and still existed between him and his mother, and finally that he might remove some or all of these difficulties by writing to his mother, who lived in a provincial city far from the capital city where he and the medical specialist lived. He was not surprised when the medical specialist agreed with this pretend-diagnosis and pretend-remedy. He, the pretender, then wrote to his mother the sort of pretend-letter that might have been written by a character in a work of fiction with a narrator not necessarily trustworthy.

The rest of this section, which is the twentieth of the thirty-four sections comprising this work of fiction, might have been written in any of a million ways, according to the epigraph of the work. I confine myself to mentioning only three of the possible million. A narrator such as narrates most of the novels, so to call them, of Thomas Hardy might report the thoughts and feelings and presentiments of the mother while she read the letter from her son and while she wrote a letter in reply; the text of each letter would, of course, be reported, as would the thoughts and feelings and presentiments of the son, the broken-down one, while he read his mother's reply. A narrator such as narrates most of the novels, so to call them, of Ernest Hemingway might report nothing of the contents of the mother's mind but much about the gestures and the grimaces and the words muttered by the son as he took his mother's letter from his letter-box and opened the envelope and read the text of the letter; much would also be reported, of course, of the thoughts and feelings and presentiments of the son while he read the letter afterwards. The narrator of this present work of fiction is one who strives to keep between his actual self and his seeming self and his seeming reader such seeming-distances as will maintain between all three personages a lasting trust. That narrator chooses to report that the son, while reading the letter and pretending to feel what a fictional son might have felt while reading a fictional letter, felt grateful to the mother for having written the sort of pretend-letter that he had expected to receive from her. He recalled while reading her letter that she had read in earlier years many books of the sort called at that time library fiction. After television had become available to her, she had no longer read books, but it seemed to the son that she had not forgotten what she had previously learned from reading books of fiction the narrators of which, he had for long supposed, were untrustworthy.

The mother's pretend-answer to the son's pretend-letter was all the excuse that the son needed for ceasing to consult the medical specialist. Yet another of his seeming or actual nervous breakdowns had seemingly or had actually come to an end before he had met up with a certain sort of female person or had read a certain work of fiction with a trustworthy narrator. In fact, the son, so to call him, only a few months after the exchange of pretend-letters with his mother, read for the first time a work of fiction that he later credited with having turned him not only into a person unlikely to break down or to seem to break down but into a person able himself to plan and to write a work of fiction. Several more years were to pass before he met up with her who seemed to be the female person he had sought to meet up with, but by then he had already written part of a work of fiction that was published some years later.

When he read for the first time the work of fiction mentioned in the sentence before the previous sentence, he was still an ignorant and gullible reader. The work was of a kind that he would have declined to read twenty years later, after he had become a discerning reader. Twenty years later he would have decided, after having read the first pages of the work, that the implied author of the work had abdicated his responsibility and had hidden himself, so to speak, behind a narrator who was self-evidently incapable of having brought the text into being. The first words of the work, which words the son mentioned above is still able to recall after not having read them for fifty years – the first words of the English translation of the original text are 'Granted that I am an inmate of a lunatic asylum...' Nowadays, he would decline to go on reading a work of fiction beginning thus, but fifty years ago he read the whole of the work mentioned and even believed himself to have learned from the work, and for the first time, that every event reported in a work of fiction is a pretend-event whether the event is reported to have taken place in the mind of a fictional personage such as Oskar Matzerath or in fictional places such as those in and around the fictional Danzig where he has his fictional existence, according to the text of *The Tin Drum*, by Günter Grass.

The word *plot* is seldom heard in the sporadic discussions that take place in this upper corridor of this remote wing of this building that remains largely unfamiliar to most of us. Many of us claim to find the word not only irrelevant but scarcely comprehensible. And yet, none of us commented derisively on the evening recently when someone reported that Charles Dickens was supposed to have laboured for days over detailed charts illustrating the sequences of fictional events in some or another work, as yet unwritten, together with the names of the characters, so to call them, who were to take part in the events and the sites where the events were to take place. In the brief silence that followed, I surmised that many of us felt a certain admiration for Charles Dickens, even though none of us would care to do what he is supposed to have done. We who avoid using the words *plot* and *character* have too much respect for those we call *fictional personages* to do more than take note of their moods and caprices, but we could hardly not admire a writer of fiction or, I should say, an implied author of fiction, who could so assert himself as to prescribe in advance what should seem to be said and done by those he might have called his characters and where and when it should thus seem. Was the implied author of the novels, so to call them, by Charles Dickens able, as none of us has ever been able, to direct the fictional behaviour of fictional personages? Or, do the so-called characters in Dickens's so-called novels have a different sort of existence from that of our personages, as we call them? Did Dickens's beings, perhaps, even lack for existence until certain words had been written with ink on paper?

On the rare occasions when we discuss authors such as
Charles Dickens, we seem to agree that we lack for something
that writers of fiction seemed formerly to possess. And yet, if we
have lost something, so to speak, we have also gained something.
We may be unable to exercise over our fictional personages
the sort of control that Dickens and others exercised over their
characters, but we are able to turn that same lack of control to
our advantage and to learn from our own subject-matter, so to
call it, in somewhat the same way that our readers are presumed
to learn from our writing.

Subject-matter and *writing*...if any of us, long ago, believed
that these two are identical or that one cannot be claimed to
exist without the other, then he would have owned to his error
soon after he had begun those simple-seeming exercises in
introspection devised at our first meetings by those of us hoping
to learn, for example, why most fictional personages seem to
behave unpredictably and not even as foreseen by those called,
for convenience, their authors. Perhaps because I had never
observed myself to do anything that might be called *thinking*,
I was at once absorbed by the exercises and learned much from
them. That which taught me most required each of us, while
writing a suitable passage in his current work, to scrutinise the
behaviour, so to call it, of some or another personage, so to call
him or her, at some or another moment, so to call it, about to
be recorded in writing. The matters at issue were as follows:
could the writer predict with certainty how the personage was
about to behave? and, if not, could the personage be said to

stand, in relation to the writer, in any way differently from some or another man or woman in the building where the writer sat writing or in the mostly level grassy countryside visible from his upper window in the building?

As I reported above, I have never seemed able to do whatever it is that other persons seem to do whenever they think or claim to be thinking. I am capable only of seeing and feeling, although I can see and feel, of course, in both the visible and the invisible worlds. Being thus disabled, I was obliged to try to answer the two questions mentioned above only by the most painstaking observation and certainly not by any rational means, whatever that phrase might denote. The sort of observation needed came easily to me. I had always considered myself the least observant of persons in the visible world, but the invisible parts of me proved able to see with acuity in the invisible world, or so I might put the matter. In summary, I learned that I have no apparent control over what sort of fictional personage might appear to me while I try to compose some or another piece of fiction. Nor am I able to decide what such a personage might do or might want to do in the invisible space surrounding him or her. All I can do is to select. This is no easy task, but I am mostly able, while struggling to keep in mind what I can only call an instinctive desire on my part to arrange the densest possible concentration of meaning on the fewest possible pages – I am mostly able to confine myself to reporting what I, whether as implied author or narrator, see fit to report.

My research, so to call it, taught me also something that

Charles Dickens and his like may not have been aware of while they planned the behaviour of those they probably called their characters. I learned how little is ever reported in fiction of all that a fictional personage is able to do or say. After having compared notes with a few like-minded residents hereabouts, I decided that I had been justified on the many occasions from as long ago as my childhood when I had wanted to read or to write – if not on paper then in my mind – the hitherto unread and unwritten reports of all that took place during the many days, weeks, or even years when certain fictional personages maintained their fictional existence although no writer had reported any detail of it.

It was no part of my research, as I call it, but often, while I was trying to hold in mind some or another personage about whom not a single word had as yet been written, I found myself speculating yet again on a matter mentioned earlier in this work of fiction. I have never been able to comprehend how the entity called in common speech *time* could be said to exist separately from the entity known likewise as *space*. To put this differently: I am unable to believe in *time* in the same way that some persons are unable to believe in a personal god. Nor does the word *space* denote for me mere extension. For me, what the word *space* denotes is hardly different from what is denoted by the word *mind*, and whenever I perform one or another of the exercises mentioned earlier, which is to say, whenever I read with due attention some or another passage of what I call true fiction or considered narration, then I become aware that the space

between each sentence and its subject-matter may well reach
endlessly in directions unknown to me.

Two men from our loose circle, so to call it, held for some years
full-time positions as teachers of creative writing in universities.
Perhaps I should have written just then that two of us admit to
having held such positions, and that others of us may prefer
not so to admit. And yet, I could hardly credit that any of us
would fear from his fellows the quiet contempt that some groups
in far parts of this building are said to hold for anyone who
formerly earned money from teaching others to write. There are
corridors, so I have heard, where residents are accorded respect
in proportion to the tens of thousands of copies of their books
sold or the numbers of their books adapted for film or even the
number of literary prizes awarded them. Most of us hereabouts
have always considered our occasional royalty payments as
bonuses or small treats while we supported ourselves and our
families by working at whatever jobs we were capable of.

Our two worked at their teaching in rather different ways,
so we have heard from them. One was resolved to disabuse his
students of any notion that the writing of fiction is a delicate
procedure to be undertaken only in silence and isolation by a
naturally sensitive person in a heightened state of alertness. This
teacher, in one of his first classes each year, after having read to
his students several passages in which one or another biographer
of D.H. Lawrence reported his writing page after page of some

or another work of fiction in the main room of the rented quarters where he and his companion lived for the time being, while the room was noisy with the conversation of the friends and admirers who seemed often to surround Lawrence, and while he himself often, and without looking up from his writing, took part in the conversation. The teacher would then stand at the whiteboard in front of his students and would begin writing with a felt-tipped pen, often pausing to amend or to erase words or phrases or whole sentences. Whenever he thus paused, he explained to the students what had caused him to pause and why he was amending or erasing. What he was writing, so he assured the students, comprised the latest hundred words and more of the work of fiction that he was then writing for publication, and he would dismiss them ten minutes early so that he could transcribe for his later use the words of his that he had written in their presence.

Our other teacher claims that he could never write so much as a sentence of fiction in the presence of another person, let alone a class of students. He writes fiction, so he says, for a few readers of good will, or perhaps for only one such reader whom he wishes never to meet but only to approach by means of his writing. Not only could he never have written fiction in front of his students, but he spoke to them about his own writing only if they had first questioned him about it. When he wanted to promote class discussions about the theory of fictional narration, as he called it, perhaps pompously, as we sometimes accuse him, although he answers that any means is justified if it earns respect for the craft

of fiction – when he wanted to promote discussion, he would put
before his students some of the large collection of statements that
he had gathered from the writings of writers themselves or from
a famous series of published interviews with writers. (It was this
collection that provided me with the epigraph for this present
work of fiction.)

The two teachers had used very different methods for assessing
the pieces of fiction written by their students. The first man relied
mostly on comments made first by the student-author and then
by his or her fellows during a detailed classroom discussion of
each piece. At the beginning of each discussion, the author would
criticise his or her piece and would then award the piece one
of the so-called grades required by the university. (The teacher
believed that this practice developed in each student the ability
to read his or her own fiction as a discerning reader might
read it.) The piece was then read by the class and afterwards
discussed. Each member of the class was required to award the
piece a grade. Finally, the teacher commented on the piece and
awarded it a grade. The final, or official, grade was the average
of all grades awarded by the class-members, the third multiple of
the author's grade, and the sixth multiple of the teacher's grade.

The other man had allowed classroom discussion of each piece
but he had always removed the author's name from the piece
before it was photocopied for reading in class. Discerning readers
in each class learned in time to identify many authors from their
distinctive styles or from the recurring subjects of their pieces,
but no member of a class was allowed to address any comment

to the author of a piece – all comments had to be written in the margins of the text as though addressed to a presumed author unlikely to be met with. The teacher himself wrote comments in the margins of each piece and would always announce his opinion of each piece to the class, but only the author of the piece learned – in writing – the grade awarded to the piece, which grade was decided by the teacher alone before he had heard any comments from anyone. He sometimes supposed that the course might be more effective if the students were never permitted to meet with each other or even with him, so that they knew each other only as the writers or the readers of certain fictional texts. His teaching methods were in keeping with his belief that the best sort of fiction had for its author not the flesh-and-blood being who might acknowledge in a classroom discussion that he or she had written this or that piece but a presumed personage whose characteristics might be something of a mystery to the flesh-and-blood being and were best recognised by a discerning reader. It was to this personage, this deep and writerly version of the author named on the title-page, that the second of the two teachers had always directed the many comments that he wrote on his students' fiction. He would never have denied that he sometimes had in mind, while he wrote the comments, an image of the author as he or she might have appeared in the classroom but he would have insisted that his words were not such as should be spoken to the person of that appearance but suitable only to be read in private by the personage responsible for his or her writing.

He had among his students each year many who were called

officially mature-age. Many of these were of his own age or older and were often the writers of the most impressive fiction. He had heard or had read of teachers in universities who had affairs with students but he had been faithfully married for nearly twenty years and was made weary by the mere thought of the deceit and the subterfuge that he would have to practise during such an affair, and he easily put off the few female students whom he supposed were signalling their interest in him. Each year, when he met his new students for the first time, he would feel himself attracted by the mere appearance of one or two of the so-called mature-age women, but he took care afterwards to deal with them no differently than he dealt with the others, which policy was usually made easier for him after those who had attracted him by their looks had failed to impress him by their writing, as almost always happened.

During his fifth year of being a teacher, he met up with circumstances the very opposite of those described in the previous sentence. The woman of all his mature-age students who attracted him most by her appearance and her deportment was also the one of all his students, whether male or female, who most impressed him by her writing. He tried to deal with her as he dealt with all his students, and according to what she told him afterwards he had mostly succeeded. Sometimes, after he had written some or another comment in the margins of some or another piece of her fiction, he felt sure that he must by now have told more than he had wanted to tell her, but even in this, so she also told him later, he had mostly succeeded also: she had found in his written words hardly more than she might have expected to find in the words of someone won over as a reader.

On the evening after the last meeting of the class that included the woman mentioned, she and her classmates, most of them mature-age, invited him to join them for drinks. The weather was very warm, and they sat under trees in semi-darkness near the cafeteria. He and she were among the last few to leave. She had drunk little, so he had observed during the evening, but he had drunk much. All of the students present had finished their undergraduate courses and expected to meet again seldom, if at all. Men and women, their teacher included, embraced one another before going their separate ways. As she later told him, he had misread her behaviour during their last minutes together, and yet he had not, so it later seemed, misread the letter that she had sent him soon after he had written to her as a result of his misreading.

They met occasionally in a hotel lounge near the building where she worked in an inner suburb, and they wrote, each of them, long letters as though trying to outdo one another in writing. Sometimes their letters included speculations about the future but they were more often concerned to interpret the past. After a certain time, she decided that they had written enough, although he felt as though much, much more demanded to be written. The few occasions when they were alone together seemed to bring her joy but they brought him nothing of the kind, which is all that he cares to report in writing about those occasions. On the last such occasion, he and she spent an afternoon in a large house of mud-brick in hilly, forested countryside north-east of the capital city. Before that day, each had talked sometimes of leaving his or her family: she her husband and daughter; he his wife and two sons. The house of mud-brick would be empty for a year while the owners were in Europe, and he and she might have spent their first year together on a forested hillside not far from the terminus of a suburban railway line. During the afternoon in the mud-brick house, each came to acknowledge that they would not meet again although they might well write to one another for many more years, which, in fact, they did.

He still recalls many of the details that occurred to him while he read for the first time a piece of fiction of hers written while she was his student and awarded by him the highest possible grade. He learned from her comments during the classroom discussion that the fiction, as he had supposed, was drawn from the author's experience, which was a guarded form of words often used in the writing class to warn readers against supposing the text in question to be mere autobiography. The chief character of the piece of fiction is a young woman, hardly more than a girl, who spent her early years in a bleak district in the north-east of England before leaving home to live and work in London. She arrives in London at a time during the late 1960s when the city is sometimes called Swinging London.

The only piece of his own published fiction that might be understood as connected with her has for its fictional setting a house on a forested hillside where a group of writers of fiction is attending a series of writers' workshops in which they read and comment on one another's fiction. The writers taking part bind themselves by the strictest of rules. No one speaks to another during their days together in the house. During workshop sessions, all comments, even those made by the supervisor, are written in silence and later distributed as photocopies. No one looks into the face of another or signals to another or groans or sighs or laughs in the hearing of another. Anyone breaking any of these or other such rules is expelled at once from the house. In the early paragraphs of the piece of fiction, the first-person narrator seems several times to refer to the recent expulsion from the house of a female person for whom the rules were seemingly too much to bear.

Even one or another discerning reader might have supposed by now that we live permanently up here in our out-of-the-way eyrie. While it would be possible for a certain sort of writer to make his home here, and a few are rumoured to have tried from time to time, everyone that I know in this corridor and those few from lower corridors whom I speak to sometimes in the grounds – each of them has another sort of home elsewhere; has a wife, perhaps, or children or grandchildren and cares and concerns very different from those that trouble him while he sits at his desk behind his upper window.

Do we never write about those concerns, those children, or those wives? I suspect that most of us do so write, although we hardly ever discuss that writing or offer it for publication.

We have not only desks in our rooms but filing cabinets: solid, steel, old-fashioned filing cabinets with locks and keys. If I surmise rightly, then many a filing cabinet will be unlocked one day in accordance with the Last Will of the man who sat for much of his life at the desk nearby – many a filing cabinet will be unlocked and many a page will be found there of a sort of writing rather different from that which covers most of the pages of this work of fiction. What did the writing-students say often of their pieces, according to the narrator of the previous section? 'This fiction is drawn from the author's experience.'

But why are we so reticent? Has not many a well-known writer seemed to make a sort of fiction out of his hating his father or divorcing his wife or watching his child endure a fatal illness? I believe us to be not so much reticent as properly respectful of, or even in awe of, what most of us hereabouts call true fiction. Even though none of us would claim to understand the matter, we sense that true fiction, the sort of fiction that we go on trying to write during year after year in this building, could never include the mere jottings of a person seeming to recall some or another painful experience of not long before. We sense that true fiction is more likely to include what was overlooked or ignored or barely seen or felt at the time of its occurrence but comes continually to mind ten or twenty years afterwards not on account of its having long ago provoked passion or pain but because of its appearing to be part of a pattern of meaning that extends over much of a lifetime.

Perhaps that is why we return continually to this towering

monstrosity, as it surely appears to some who see it from a distance and never know what goes on in its many wings and behind its many windows. Perhaps that is why each of us looks up often while he steers his car across the mostly level countryside hereabouts, waiting to see the glowing of late sunlight in the windows of his true home. Perhaps each of us, whenever he returns yet again to his upper room and passes the row of locked filing cabinets on his way to his desk – perhaps each of us hears in mind at such a time not the cautious phrases of some or another posthumous biography but the manifold rhythms of one after another subordinate clause in quite another sort of book. Perhaps each of us is driven most urgently not by his wanting to be the subject of some or another biography and not even by his wanting to be the author of some or another memorable volume but by his wanting to grasp the paradox that has exercised him during much of his lifetime: by his wanting to understand how the so-called actual and the so-called possible – what he did and what he only dreamed of doing – come finally to be indistinguishable in the sort of text that we call true fiction.

Every one of us in this remote series of rooms would have fallen in love with more than a few fictional female personages. Leaving aside the question what is meant by the expression *to fall in love*, I can surely add that each of us finds himself equally liable to fall in love with the sort of personage who appears to him while he reads some or another fictional text or the sort of personage who appears to him from out of the space between fictional texts and whom he then seeks to have as a personage in a text of his own making. One of us, so I happened to learn recently while we two alone were drinking late – one of us had, nearly thirty years ago, the experience of falling in love with an entity, so to call her, who was both an actual female person, one of the sumless inhabitants of the spaces between fictional texts, and also a seeming likeness, if not the embodiment, of a personage who had first appeared to him nearly ten years before while he was reading a work of non-fiction first published nearly ten years before his birth, which personage was also a fictional personage in a work of fiction that he was writing at the time when he fell in love, so to speak, with the entity, so to call her.

I offer no apology to any sort of reader for any difficulties that he or she may have had with the previous sentence. Some of us in this topmost storey have been, or are still, entangled in such matters as cannot be reported in simple sentences. We are, during all our waking hours, rememberers of what we have read or have written, lamenters of what we have failed to read or write, projectors of what we hope still to read or to write, and breathing men, able, despite our many other concerns, to pace these corridors or to stroll through the grounds around this building or to travel whither we choose in the mostly level countryside beyond the grounds and no less likely than any other sort of man to fall in love with someone seen from a distance or met up with.

The man who is the chief character of this and several

surrounding paragraphs read for the first time, early in his fifth decade, a book of non-fiction, so to call it, reporting, among many other matters, the death of a young woman, hardly more than a girl, who had leaped into a well on a remote farming estate comprising mostly level grassy countryside in the south-west of the Kingdom of Hungary more than thirty years before his birth. As is often the way with us frequenters of this upper corridor, the man, some ten years after he had first read the book mentioned, had set out to write a work of fiction in order not only to explain to himself why the image of a certain young woman, hardly more than a girl, was constantly in his mind but also to learn, if it were possible, what he seemed required to learn whenever the image seemed, as it often seemed, to importune him. He knew about the young woman, hardly more than a girl, who was mentioned in the first sentence of this paragraph and was mentioned in only three paragraphs of the book of non-fiction mentioned there, only that she had leaped into the well after having run during the night from the bedroom of the farm-overseer, her employer; that she had been unusually good-looking, although when her corpse had been dragged from the well and had been laid on the frozen soil nearby, her face had been disfigured by scratches caused, perhaps, by the buckets of the cowherds who had discovered her when they were watering their cattle at dawn; and that she had leaped barefoot into the well, having left her boots behind in her haste to leave the bedroom of the farm-overseer, her employer.

When he set out to write the work of fiction mentioned above, the man with the image constantly in his mind knew no more about the young woman mentioned above than what is reported about her in the previous sentence. He did not know, for example, what was the colour of her hair or what was her name. Of what might be called her history he knew only that she had left her boots in the bedroom of the farm-overseer, her employer. The man knew, however, a great deal about the image-person, so to call her. He knew that she was dark-haired; he knew her name; and he had learned, in somewhat the way that a person learns such matters in dreams, much about her history, as it might be called.

I ought, perhaps, to have repeated in each of the previous two sentences not that the chief character of these paragraphs *knew* certain matters but that he *seemed to know* them or that he *claimed to know* them. I wrote what I wrote after having recalled certain discussions between the chief character and myself, his narrator for the time being. We in this isolated corridor hold many views considered eccentric in other parts of the building, but even we find extreme and untenable some of the claims of the chief character. He claims to believe, for example, that the image-person, as I called her above, did not come into being as a result of his having read a certain three paragraphs in a certain book of non-fiction but that she pre-existed that event and that his taking-in with his eyes the text of the three paragraphs was merely the event that enabled him and her to meet up with one another. He even claims to believe that an image-person may be sometimes capable of influencing textual events, by which he seems to mean that his dark-haired image-person might not only have caused a certain three paragraphs of text to be written but might somehow have influenced him, nearly fifty years later, to become a reader of those paragraphs.

We, the colleagues, so to call us, of this speculator, so to call him, have for long agreed that the reading and the writing of texts, even of so-called non-fiction texts, are mysterious processes indeed. Some of us talk without awkwardness of an invisible world inhabited by the beings who appear to us while we read. We acknowledge that the invisible beings seem largely independent of us and even that they are able to affect our thinking and our behaviour, but the speculator, my chief character, would have us believe rather more than this.

At some time during the two and more years while he was writing the work of fiction last mentioned in the paragraph preceding the previous paragraph, the chief character, as I call him, who was already the author of several published books of fiction, was invited by some or another body to be one of a number of writer-guests at the annual conference of the body, which had as its stated aim the study of the literature of the chief character's native country. He, the chief character, was about to draft a polite apology for his not attending before he learned that the conference was to take place in the island-state that was the southern-most state of his native country. He had never cared to travel, but he had long been curious about certain parts of the island-state, especially the district known as the Midlands, which he believed to comprise mostly level grassy countryside, and so he accepted the invitation. He travelled by boat to the island-state and then by car to the conference. He recalled afterwards that he had read a few pages from one of his published works, at a session of the conference when several writers thus read, but he recalled little else. He had been made uneasy by the strangeness of his surroundings and had been drunk or hung-over during most of the conference.

At one time while he was hung-over and was eating breakfast, or it may have been lunch, in the cafeteria where the other conference-attendees were also eating, he noticed a certain dark-haired young woman at a nearby table. He judged from the appearance of the young woman that one or both of her parents may have been Hungarian. Most of the persons in the cafeteria knew one another, if only by name, and he was able to learn from someone at his table the name of the young woman, which was not a Hungarian name, and that she was a member of the English Department at a university campus in a provincial city of his own state.

The chief character of these paragraphs has never written any piece of fiction drawing on any experience of his from the few months after he had met the dark-haired young woman at the conference in the island-state. He offers as his reason that he wrote, during the last week of that period, a long letter that could itself be considered a work of fiction, so shapely is it and so full of meaning. The original of the letter was sent to the dark-haired young woman, but the writer of the letter has kept a copy and is not unwilling to have it read and appraised by others of our group. The letter comprises more than twenty-five thousand words and was written at several different places in the island-state, whither the writer of the letter went a second time only a few months after he had met there with the dark-haired young woman and on the day following a meeting with the young woman, at which meeting both had seemed to understand that they would not meet again.

The author of the letter that might be called a work of fiction avoids using the word *coincidence*. He claims that a person who writes fiction of meaning or who reads such fiction with discernment is able to recognise that the details of what we call our lives go sometimes to form patterns of meaning not unlike those to be found in our preferred sort of fiction. He claims that the word *coincidence* was far from occurring to him only weeks after his first visit to the island-state, when he received a second invitation to visit there. The body inviting him had no connection with the association that had previously invited him. His second visit took the form of an organised tour during which he and two female writers conducted so-called writers' workshops each afternoon and stayed each night in a motel or in bed-and-breakfast accommodation. He had dinner each evening with the other writers but then went to his room and continued writing his letter.

On the evening before the last day of the tour, he had still not finished his letter. It was important to him that the last words of the letter should be written somewhere in the island-state and that the parcel enclosing the letter should bear a postmark of the island-state. On the last day of the tour, he and the other two writers were to travel by car from the south to the north-west of the state, there to set out homewards. He could not think of trying to finish his letter in the car, with the women watching him, but towards noon the others decided that they had time enough to visit a certain so-called historic building in the district known as the Midlands. They had been travelling for some time across mostly level grassy countryside with a range of forested mountains in the distance on either side. At what he chose to consider the very centre of the mostly level district, they turned aside into the spacious grounds of a building of two, or it may have been three, storeys. He told the others that he was unwell and would rest in the car, but as soon as they had left the car he took out his letter and wrote. While the others were, presumably, touring the building of two, or it may have been three storeys, he was able to finish the last few paragraphs of the letter. Several times, it seemed to him as though some or another person was looking out at him from one or another of the upper windows, but whenever he looked towards the windows he saw only one after another reflection in the glass of some or another part of the sky, which was filled with grey-white clouds.

I have looked into the letter, although not recently. It seems partly an account of all that had taken place between the writer and the dark-haired young woman, who was twenty years his junior, during the few months before the letter was begun: his finding a pretext for introducing himself to her at the conference where he first saw her; his learning at their first meeting that she had taught, as she expressed it, one of his books to undergraduates; his asking for her postal address and soon afterwards writing to her what he called warm letters; her answering some of his letters, often with her own form of warmth; their meeting several times in the lounge-bar of one or another hotel in the capital city or in the provincial city where she lived; and finally, after his having decided (wrongly, as he claimed in a parenthetical passage) that he had written enough to her (for he had gone on writing no less frequently even after they had begun meeting in lounge-bars), their meeting on two occasions in a stone cottage used sometimes by her parents in a district that he had never previously visited, which was a district of mostly undulating grassy countryside and shallow, gravelly creeks flowing towards the inland from the Great Dividing Range. The text seems to suggest that neither meeting brought joy to him or to her and that the second meeting was the occasion when both seemed to understand that they would not meet again, although he might well write to her once more, which, as we know, he did.

I used the adverb *partly* in the second sentence of the previous paragraph. The document summarised in that paragraph seems partly a detailed report of the matters mentioned in that paragraph and partly a letter – but a letter intended not so much for the person addressed at the head of the first page as for someone known, perhaps, only to the writer. I noticed at once, when I first looked into the letter, that the writer uses the third-person form of every verb. That is to say, he addresses no person directly but writes as most authors of fiction write, reporting fictional events, some of them seemingly actual, for the seeming-benefit of a personage who might be called his reader-in-mind or his implied reader. I was often persuaded, while I read, that this possible or ideal reader is someone long dead.

The author of the letter, as I reported earlier, declines to use the word *coincidence* which, so he claims, is used by persons unwilling to allow that some events seem more likely to be part of a narrative than merely to have happened. The author, in his letter, makes much of the young literature tutor's having the dark hair and even the sort of complexion common among Hungarian persons. He makes even more of her having a small scar on her cheek. He makes still more of her having bought for him, before his first visit to the stone cottage in the mostly undulating grassy countryside, a pair of boots known as gumboots, so that he noticed, as soon as he had arrived at the cottage, two pairs of black boots standing together at the back door. (He and she later wore the boots while they walked together through the damp paddocks around the cottage and then through the shallow creek to the forest nearby.) In the passages that I looked at, the author makes no direct claim but he sometimes writes as though he credits the young woman mentioned much earlier in these paragraphs – the young woman who died more than thirty years before his birth – with an achievement that is surely possible only for a certain sort of fictional personage and then only in the invisible space between the fictional and the actual; as though he supposes that the personage long dead had somehow reached him through the agency of the dark-haired tutor of literature; and as though he is far from complaining that his and her affair, so to call it, ended as it did but accepts this as an appropriate punishment for his having wanted more than the singular satisfaction previously available to him in the invisible space mentioned.

Those books that I mentioned in a much earlier section of this work – those books on the so-called techniques of fiction – all include a section devoted to *dialogue,* and yet I cannot recall having heard that word uttered in any of the many discussions held hereabouts during my many years in this building. Even an undiscerning reader would have understood by now that our sort of writer avoids the use of dialogue or so-called direct speech in his fiction because it gives to a text the appearance of a filmscript or a playscript. Many a one of us would have both a personal reason and what might be called a theoretical reason for not wanting even to discuss film or live theatre, so to call it. Such a one would prefer not to recall the glaring images and the shouted exchanges and the intrusive music from the cinemas where he wasted whole afternoons or evenings during his childhood. He is equally reluctant to recall the theatres where he sat tensely beside some or another young woman whom he had *asked out*, to use the jarring expression of those years, while he struggled to identify what he supposed was the meaning of the play or the issues that it addressed – not for his own satisfaction but so that he could announce them later to the young woman as a demonstration of his intellectual or cultural acquirements.

Such a one would prefer not to recall the young man who had supposed that a few hours spent staring at a flickering screen or a half-lit stage were in some way comparable with the experience of reading even twenty pages of true fiction.

As for the so-called theoretical reason mentioned above, many a one of us, having opened by chance some or another work of fiction, turns away from the sight of quotation marks looking like swarms of flies or a series of dashes like rungs on a ladder to nowhere – he turns away because dialogue, so to call it, is of all the tricks and devices used by writers of fiction that which most readily persuades the undiscerning reader that the purpose of fiction is to provide the nearest possible equivalents of experiences obtainable in this, the visible world where books are written and read. Many a young writer must often be tempted to compose a passage of dialogue rather than struggle with a report of elusive or abstruse matters. Suppose such a writer to be trying to write a fictional account of the death of a grandparent of the chief character. (Those of us who once earned a living as teachers of creative writing, so to call it, tell me that many a younger student was able to write a piece of fiction of considerable meaning about this sort of occasion, which was often the presumed author's first experience of the death of someone close.) The young writer surely has in mind images of rooms and of furniture or of scenery out of doors; images of persons speaking and gesturing, images of scents, perhaps from a garden or from a corridor in a hospital; images of sensations such as the feel of wind against his face or of breasts encased in

fabric while his mother holds him against herself. The writer
wants to compose from these seeming memories such sentences
as will seem to bring to the reader what he or she would call an
actual experience. The writer seeks words for those sentences,
but words, as he would have learned already, are not so readily
available as are seeming memories and the like. But then there
occurs to the writer a means of filling his pages much more
rapidly than he could have filled them with sentences laboriously
composed. The writer is able to recall whole sequences of words
that he first heard on the occasion of his grandparent's death.
What he recalls are, in fact, not words but images of words.
Images of words, however, unlike images of scenery, say, or of
the feel of breasts encased in fabric seem to most persons so like
the words themselves as to be hardly distinguishable. And so, the
young writer, while he seems to hear, clearly and unmistakably,
many a sequence of words that was once uttered in his hearing or
that he himself once uttered – the young writer is able to fill space
after blank space on his pages with words such as the following.

'Why are you crying, Mother?' I asked.

'You'll have to be strong, son,' she replied. 'Your pa has gone
to heaven.'

This paragraph has been written for the benefit of any person
who may have picked up this work of fiction in a bookshop or
in any other surroundings and who may have opened the work
at this page and who may have read immediately afterwards the
previous two lines and may then have assumed that other similar
lines appear on many of the surrounding pages. No other such

lines appear anywhere in this work of fiction or in any of the works of fiction written in this out-of-the-way corridor of this vast building. We who have found our way to this outpost, as it might be called – we not only consider dialogue, as it is called, the crudest of the many devices used by those writers of fiction whose chief aim is to have their readers believe they are not reading a work of fiction, but we ourselves have it as *our* chief aim that our readers should be continually mindful that what they are reading is nothing else *but* fiction.

And yet...how often are we obliged to write those words after an expression of a forthright belief? Perhaps forty years ago, when I was still forming my judgements in many matters, I read of a writer whose novels, as they were called, consisted almost wholly of dialogue. I recall her name, which was Ivy Compton-Burnett, and that she was an eccentric female solitary. Did I learn also that she lived alone in a house of two, or perhaps three, storeys in the English countryside? Or, am I too much influenced by what I have in mind while I write these pages? Certainly, I read one of her works of fiction, which consisted, sure enough, of dialogue and little else. Not surprisingly, I have forgotten almost everything that I experienced while I read the work. I have not forgotten, however, a mental image of a large house of stone, almost as imposing as the wing where I sit writing these words. The house is occupied by an uncertain number of personages, many of whom seem to be siblings or near-relations and unmarried. These personages seem to meet up with one another at unpredictable times and to discuss, among other

GERALD MURNANE

matters, difficulties between themselves and their parents. At
other times, they seem to wander through the house of stone,
talking at length but often as though to themselves. One such
personage is named Horace. He is the only personage whose
name I recall. He may also be the only personage who seemed,
while I read, to be more than a mere utterer of dialogue, so to
call it. Horace is reported in the text as having spoken the only
words that I recall from the whole book of fiction. He speaks
the words, as I recall, on one of the occasions when a number
of personages are reported as trying to explain to one another
why they are obliged to live under such harsh conditions. One of
them is reported as saying something such as 'Oh, well, a man's
a man.' Horace is then reported as saying something such as
'That is not so. I am not.'

One of those two who formerly taught writing in universities
once made what he calls a detailed study of the subject-matter
of all the pieces of fiction that had earned from him, during
the previous two years, the grade of High Distinction. He had
already observed, before he began his study, that almost every
piece of fiction that impressed him, regardless of the manner
of its narration, included what he chose to call a chief character
and a lesser character and that the interest of the fiction arose
out of the dealings between these two. When he began his study,
the teacher had not yet decided how to classify the many sorts
of chief character and lesser character that he was likely to find.

He supposed that he might classify the characters first according to their gender and then according to their relatedness with one another, as, for example, wife and husband, mother and son, friend and friend, and the like. He was only a little way into his study when he decided that all such relationships were divisible into two groups only: relationships determined by blood and those otherwise determined. He then set about separating the pieces of fiction under study according to this division. The results surprised him somewhat. He had expected that a majority of the pieces would have included characters from the second of the two groups, but the opposite was the result. In nearly two thirds of the pieces of fiction that had impressed him during the two years past, the most prominent characters were blood-relations. It then occurred to him that he could further divide these pairs of characters into two groups. In one group were those pairs whose relationship might be called vertical, as, for example, parents and children, while the other group comprised those related horizontally, as, for example, siblings or cousins. Again, one group outnumbered the other, this time even more so: in about four fifths of the pieces, the relationship between the chief characters was the so-called vertical.

I heard about this study long ago, and I recalled it recently when I was conducting what might be called a simple study of my own. Some of us, of course, can never be induced, even during long drinking-sessions, to reveal any detail of their latest fictional projects, their works-in-hand. Others talk freely about their writerly tasks, even if only, as some of them claim, so that their talking will rid them of what was fit only for gossip and will leave them with the deep, stubborn matter needed for giving shape to sentences and paragraphs. The reported subject-matter of two such projects deserves to be included in this, my own latest work. Of course, I have seen not a single page of either project, but I am so used to assembling texts-in-the-mind from scant impressions that the following paragraphs may seem as though I lately read the originals or even wrote them.

The first-person narrator of the first of the two projects claims, in its first pages, to recall the details of certain Sunday afternoons, perhaps fifty years earlier, in a large house of stone with a spacious formal garden in a provincial city on the south-west coast of the state in which he was born. The discerning reader will have been pleased to note the verb *claims* in the previous sentence and will have understood rightly that the piece of fiction is far from being one of those so-called re-creations of the past that are written in the present tense, presumably so that the reader will be required to do no more than to watch a sort of filmic mental imagery while his or her eyes scan the text. No, the narrator not only *claims* to recall certain details but also reflects on them, which tells me that the author of the text is in favour of considered narration as I defined it in the third paragraph of the sixth section of this present work of fiction. The first-person narrator of the text in question reflects on some of the impressions made on him during the Sunday afternoons mentioned when he was a visitor in the large house of stone and when it was visited also by four other persons.

The head of the house of stone was the widowed mother of the father of the narrator. The other persons living in the house were one of the three sons and three of the four daughters of the widow, and were, of course, an uncle and three aunts of the narrator. None of these four persons had ever married. The son had courted several young women but had not persisted for long in his courtships. One of the daughters had been courted, but her suitor had not persisted for long. During the years when the piece of fiction was set, so to speak, all four single persons might have been described as approaching middle age and might have been considered likely to remain single. The narrator, being what I call a strong and a consciously knowledgeable narrator, is able to inform his reader, at an early point in the narration, that the four single persons would, in fact, remain single throughout their lives, even though the action of the fiction takes place, so to speak, long before the lives of the four have ended.

The four other visitors mentioned in a recent paragraph were three brothers and a sister, all of whom might have been described as middle-aged. Their mother had been a sister of the father of the four single residents of the house of stone, meaning that the eight were all first cousins. None of the four visitors had ever married. The narrator did not know whether or not any of the three men-visitors had ever conducted a courtship or the single woman-visitor had been courted, but he supposed that all four were likely to remain always single and, as the narrator did not hesitate to inform the reader, his supposition had later been proved correct. The four visitors, like the four residents, lived together in a large house although with no parent for company, both of their parents having died long before. Another difference between the two groups of four was that the house where the visitors lived was of brick rather than of stone and was far larger than the stone house, being of two storeys with dormer windows in the upper storey. The large house of brick was at a distance from the house of stone and was at a distance also from the coast. The dormer windows of the house of brick overlooked mostly level grassy countryside on the southern margins of the extensive plains in the south-west of the state where all nine of the fictional personages, together with the narrator, had been born.

On the few Sunday afternoons that the narrator claimed to recall, he was a young man, hardly more than a boy, sitting quietly in the background in the dining-room of the house of stone while his widowed grandmother and his three unmarried aunts cleared the table after the midday meal and served tea. (The persons in the dining-room abstained almost wholly from alcohol, although not from any religious conviction.) The talk would have been lively enough during the meal, but while they drank tea the eight cousins reached the peak of their achievements as wits and conversationalists, or so it seemed at the time to the narrator. He, in the person of the narrator of the fiction, reported a few of the anecdotes and exchanges that he claimed to recall. (He reported them of course, always indirectly and in summary; he was writing fiction and not a script for the cinema or the theatre.) He acknowledged that his reports could not bring to the mind of even a discerning reader the mood, so to call it, that overhung the dining-table on those long-ago Sundays in the house of stone. But he reminded his readers that such was not his task; that he was narrating a piece of true fiction and was required to do no more and no less than to report the contents of his mind, among which were his recollections of how he had seemed to feel on those Sundays. And about those recollections he wrote eloquently enough for me.

Their being unmarried allowed the eight cousins more time and more energy to stand apart from their social setting, so to call it, and to see more clearly and to comment more sharply on the follies of their neighbours and their acquaintances. They even dared, they who might never have fallen in love, to mock – although not too unkindly – the troubles, as they saw them, of those who courted or were courted. Above all, they who were comparatively prosperous, having only themselves to provide for, scorned what they called materialism, which meant for them mostly the advertising of goods for which they had no need. Only one item of human behaviour was never mentioned and seldom even hinted at during the exchanges that stayed in the mind of the narrator for perhaps fifty years. Every person in the room seemed at pains to avoid any sort of acknowledgement of what might be called sexuality.

The young man, hardly more than a boy, who sat in the background mostly admired the persons who kept up their banter around the dining table. He even came close, at times, he for whom sexuality and falling in love seemed cruel punishments rather than any sort of pleasure – he even came close to wanting to become one of them: to saving all the effort that he expended on searching for images of sexually provoking females or actual dark-haired females suitable for falling in love with and to converting that effort into the sort of energy that would give rise continually to jokes and witticisms and to his feeling that he had escaped from the turmoil that beset most persons and was free to look down, as it were, from an upper window and across a mostly level grassy landscape, at the wretches who lusted after one another or fell in love with one another.

Only a few years after the young man, hardly more than a boy, had felt as was reported above, he felt far otherwise. He had gone back to falling in love and to relieving his sexual urges, so to call them, and he considered the persons who had slapped their thighs and had shrieked and laughed around the dining table to be mental cripples. His, the narrator's, having set out to write the piece of fiction summarised in these paragraphs, came from a suspicion, if not a change of heart, that had occurred to him in recent years. If he was not quite ready to believe it, then he suspected, at the time when he was older by several years than the oldest of the unmarrieds had been when he had first sat among them, that those who had thumped the table and had guffawed were not at all to be pitied or condemned; that they might have sensed, early in life, that so much was at risk if ever they should fall in love, let alone make sexual contact with another – so much was at risk that they had better remain heart-whole, to use that allusive term. He suspected that they had decided, early in life, that no one was to be trusted.

I referred in an earlier paragraph of this section to a second piece of fiction that I was able recently to appraise from among the largely unknown pieces going forward in this upper corner of this vast and confusing edifice. The narrator of that second piece – again a first-person narrator – refers frequently to a book of non-fiction first published when he was a young man, rather more than a boy. The book reports that a certain anthropologist in the state of California read in a newspaper in the early years of the twentieth century that a so-called wild man had been captured recently in a township in a remote forested district in the north of the state. The anthropologist travelled to the township and learned, with the help of a translator, that the wild man, so to call him, was the last survivor of a group of Native Americans who had persisted furtively in their way of life all throughout the nineteenth century while their territory was being encroached on by farmers and by roads and railways. The group had survived, although barely, in the forested margins of the settled districts until they numbered only a male and two females. The male was he who was reported in the newspaper as being a captive wild man, although he had not been captured but had approached the township mentioned after the two females, his last remaining companions, had died and he had become the only survivor of his people.

The anthropologist arranged for the last survivor, so to call him, to be accommodated at his, the anthropologist's, university in a suite of rooms adapted to his needs. Until the survivor died from an infectious disease some ten years later, he lived

GERALD MURNANE

contentedly, or so it seemed. He learned the language of his
rescuers; he dressed as they dressed; and the book in which
these matters are reported includes even a reproduction of a
photograph of the survivor seated and smiling in a private box
during a theatrical performance.

The first-person narrator who was last mentioned early in the
paragraph preceding the previous paragraph reported that an
earlier version of himself, so to call him, had been so affected by
his having read about the last survivor, so to call him, that he, the
earlier version, had planned to write a work of fiction the chief
character of which would be a young man, rather more than a
boy, who was obliged to live in surroundings utterly uncongenial
to him, almost as though he was himself the last survivor of
some or another sort of extinct people. The work of fiction that
I referred to earlier as the second work of fiction is largely an
account of the chief character's trying to write the work of fiction
mentioned in the previous sentence.

The last survivor, so to call him, took pleasure from
demonstrating to the anthropologist and his colleagues the
details of his, the survivor's, previous way of life, so to call it:
how his people had built their dwelling-places and had obtained
their food and had made their clothes and utensils and weapons;
what might be called their religious beliefs; and, of course, their
language. The survivor, however, would never reveal his name,
which had been a secret between himself and a few others.
He was known to the anthropologist and his colleagues by the
word that was the equivalent of *man* in the language of the

162

perished people. One other matter the man, as I should now call him, would never discuss. Although he explained in outline the customs or conventions of his people in matters such as courtship and their forms of betrothal and marriage, he would never reply to any question about his own personal history. Of the two female persons who had been his last companions until they had died, one was much older than he while the other was of about his own age. Whenever the anthropologist would try to learn what relationship, if any, existed between the man and the women and would even question whether he and one or another of them had been sexual partners, the man would fall resolutely silent and would blush. The anthropologist surmised that the older woman might have been the mother of the man while the younger might have been what might be called some sort of cousin: a member of a clan or sub-group that he was forbidden from approaching, even if he and she might have been the last of their people on earth.

It was wonderful how she felt, by the time she had seen herself through this narrow pass, that she had really achieved something – that she was emerging a little in fine, with the prospect less contracted. She had done for him, that is, what her instinct enjoined; had laid a basis not merely momentary on which he could meet her. When, by the turn of his head, he did finally meet her, this was the last thing that glimmered out of his look; but it came into sight, none the less, as a perception of his distress and almost as a question of his eyes; so that, for still another minute,

GERALD MURNANE

before he committed himself, there occurred between them a kind of unprecedented moral exchange over which her superior lucidity presided...

We may seem, to some of the other factions and groupings in this huge building, as though we are sure of ourselves: as though we long ago worked out our position in matters fictional and have never since wavered. We are, however, as liable as any other group with a policy to feel sometimes as though we restrict ourselves unduly, or, at least, as though we need encouragement of some sort. Especially when one of us has pointed out to the others a paragraph in a newspaper reporting that a valuable literary prize has been awarded to a person known to us as incapable of composing a shapely sentence, or when one of us has read a so-called review of one of his books blaming him for seeming to avoid crucial moral and social issues – especially at such a time will many a one of us try to cheer himself by doing as I did a few minutes ago when I reached for the nearest of my collection of books with Henry James for their author, let the pages fall apart wherever they might, and then read aloud one or another of the many passages there that might have suited my purposes.

None of us has ever claimed to feel much affinity for the man of flesh and blood who went by the name of Henry James and who died nearly a century ago. I doubt whether any of us knows more than a few details of the life or the character of that man. All of us, though, feel a comradeship with the personage seemingly responsible for the texts of the works of fiction with Henry James for their author. We see that personage as the exemplar of what we call the strong narrator: a personage who has never sought to hide behind his or her subject-matter as the author of a filmscript or playscript hides but who seems to stride defiantly to and fro between his or her subject-matter and the reader, asserting his or her right to be the sole interpreter of that subject-matter, so that we seem to see or to hear, while we read, not the pretend-deeds or the pretend-words of persons pretending to be actual persons but the measured sentences of true fiction: sentences reporting what no one but the narrator has seen or heard in the invisible setting where all fiction takes place.

I have already betrayed, as an accepted habit, and even to extravagance commented on, my preference for dealing with my subject-matter, for 'seeing my story', through the opportunity and the sensibility of some more or less detached, some not strictly involved, though thoroughly interested and intelligent, witness or reporter, some person who contributes to the case mainly a certain amount of criticism and interpretation of it.

The above is a mere fragment from the most astonishing account of fictional narration that I have read or expect ever to read. The account, as I call it, is the Preface that Henry James wrote for *The Golden Bowl* when that work was published in 1909 as part of the so-called New York edition of his works. One of our group has learned by heart not only the passage above but several other long extracts from the Preface. He tells us that he recites one or more of the passages aloud whenever he needs to remind himself that the task of fictional narration is no mere drudgery prescribed in advance by the seeming solidity of its subject but an undertaking to be compared with the drafting of a musical composition for full orchestra. If the same man, however, at some or another gathering of ours, seems likely to begin one of his recitations, a certain one of us will always leave the room in order not to hear words that frighten him, so he says, rather than inspire him. He once read a large part of the Preface, so he tells us, and next day, at his desk, was scarcely able to write, so hindered was he by the continual suspicion that he might not have the right amount of sensibility or detachment, or that he might be too involved, or not enough interested or intelligent or not able to contribute the right amount of criticism or interpretation. This fearful fellow, however, is an exception among us. We others will often call on our memoriser to recite for us, and often, after we have heard him to the end, and especially if we are drinking, will take to the floor ourselves, with one after another reading aloud his favourite passage from his favourite work of Henry James and struggling to make himself heard above such cries from his audience as 'Go, you champion narrator!' and 'You tell 'em, Harry!'

We have another use for the fictional texts of Henry James: we use them as an exercise, a sort of parlour game, on evenings when our writing has tired us. We choose a set number of pages from the one text, say the pages of *The Golden Bowl* numbered from 100 to 150 inclusive in the Penguin edition of 1966. Then we compete during a given time, which is never less than an hour, to find in those pages the greatest number of passages in which the seeming third-person narrator reveals, by even as little as a word or a phrase, that he is, in fact, a first-person narrator, or, to use the terms of the passage quoted above, that behind the thoroughly interested witness or reporter stands always a sort of ghostly narrator such as is found often in James's works but seldom elsewhere.

We could hardly be said to read the texts while we search. We perform a sort of scanning, alert always to key words of phrases more often, though not always, likely to appear at the beginnings of sentences. While I was making notes for this paragraph in this present work of fiction, I found, during an hour spent in scanning the fifty-one pages mentioned above, four examples of what I was looking for. On page 111 I found this passage: 'We share this world, none the less, for the hour, with Mr Verver...' I found this on page 130: 'That, none the less, was but a flicker; what made the real difference, as I have hinted, was his mute passage with Maggie.' I found this on the very next page: 'So much mute communication was doubtless, all this time, marvellous, and we may confess to having read into the scene, prematurely, a critical character that took longer to develop.' Finally, I found on page 135 the following passage, which might well be subject to dispute: 'The extent to which they enjoyed their indifference to any judgement of their want of ceremony, what did that of itself speak but for the way that, as a rule, they almost equally had others on their mind?'

We could hardly be called a demonstrative group but sometimes, late of an evening, when one of us has learned that he was the only one of all of us to have identified a certain brief passage of self-conscious narration, so to call it, in fifty or a hundred pages of the fiction of the Master, as some of us choose to call him, he, the lone identifier, will raise his glass of beer and will utter the sort of cry more likely to be heard when a football match or a horse-race is close to its end, mostly, we others suppose, in order to celebrate his prowess as a student of fictional narration but also, we like to hope, as a tribute to the richness of texts properly narrated.

Some of us play what might be called textual games not only in competition with one another but also alone and in private. One of us has sometimes mentioned an elaborate game that he first devised as a young man, hardly more than a boy, in order to decide the positions of various imaginary racehorses, so to call them, at successive points during imaginary races, so to call them, and, finally, at the winning post. The deviser of the game is mostly reticent about it. We know that he has played his game during most of his life, although we do not know how much of his time he devotes to it and how much more fiction he might have written if he had never been seduced by the game. We do not know, for example, when one of us sees him from the lawns below standing at his window and staring far past us for a few moments before returning to his desk – we do not know whether we have caught him straining to visualise one after another possible ending to some or another half-run horse-race in his mind or struggling to arrange the ending to some or another half-composed sentence of fiction in his mind. Nor do we know, when we hear from our corridor, as sometimes happens, the repeated thumping of his fist on his desk-top, whether he is celebrating his having composed, after much struggle, a sentence comprising numerous clauses or the arrival at the winning-post and ahead of its opponents of a horse that had been buried in the ruck at the home-turn. We know that the outcome of each race depends on the occurrence of certain letters or punctuation marks or even of certain common words in passages of prose chosen by the player of the game. We had assumed until recently that these passages were chosen at random, but we were lately told by the deviser of the game that he chooses his decisive passages in strict sequence from the opening page onwards of the nineteenth-century novel *The Cloister and the Hearth*, by Charles Reade. He had stolen an edition of this book, so he once told me, from a dusty upstairs library managed by a group of grey-haired women. Or, the book had been the last that he had borrowed from the meagre stock in the library and he had been too busy or too lazy to return it, so he told me on another occasion. His having kept the book may, in fact, be connected with a certain image of a dark-haired young woman, hardly more than a girl, in a duotone illustration among the preliminary pages of the book, which image, so he once told one of us in an unguarded moment, was the image of the daughter of a certain trainer of racehorses in a district of mostly level grassy countryside in the imaginary world, so to call it, where his imaginary races are decided.

This is almost all that we know about our colleague and his game-playing, which is probably no more odd than any other of the textual diversions that occupy some of us in private. What I find curious is that the man in question has read only a small part of the text of *The Cloister and the Hearth* and will die long before he has read to the end of it, so he has told several of us. He began to devise the elaborate rules and stratagems for his game during the first days after he had brought home from the library the book that he was never to return, and he had decided to read the text only during the hours while the game was going forward. A single race might take a whole afternoon or a whole evening to be decided and to have its results recorded in detail in the ledgers where he stores such things. But a race needs for its running only a few paragraphs of prose. Even if he were to give up writing and reading fiction and to keep mostly to his room, he would never learn the fictional fate, so to call it, of the dark-haired fictional young woman denoted by an image in the duotone illustration mentioned, and even the dark-haired daughter of the trainer of racehorses would grow older by no more than a few years during the remainder of his life.

The other of the two known game-players among us talks openly and often about his game. He devised the first, primitive version of the game when he was a young man, hardly more than a boy, much given to daydreaming about sexual adventures, so to call them, and to masturbating while images of such adventures passed through his mind. He was continually dissatisfied with the contents of his image-adventures, so to call them. The image-females were always too compliant and too obliging. He might have said about them what an undiscerning critic or reviewer might write about certain characters in some or another book under review: he might have said that the females were not convincing. As a first effort towards making the females more so, he introduced the element of chance into his sexual fantasies, so to call them. He arranged to have two possible outcomes for each attempt on his part (I mean, of course, on the part of his imagined counterpart in the fantasy) to advance his cause, so to call it. If he attempted, for example, to kiss a certain female, the two possible outcomes were that she would permit him to do so and that she would not so permit him. Which of the possible outcomes became the actual, so to call it, was determined by the number of letters, whether odd or even, in a word or a phrase that he chose for the purpose. The word or phrase had to be chosen in haste, lest he be able to estimate in advance whether it contained an odd number of letters, and would therefore result in an unfavourable outcome, or an even number leading to a favourable outcome. As a means of preventing himself from calling on a word or phrase that he knew to have an even number of letters, he took to choosing in haste a word or phrase connected with the scene in mind. If, for example, he and a female personage were imagined as being together on a deserted beach, he might decide without hesitation on the phrase *brief bathing-costume* or the phrase *bare sunburned shoulders* and then set about learning what he genuinely did not know, which was whether the phrase comprised an odd or an even number of letters. (If he had visualised the second of the two phrases quoted as having a comma between the two adjectives, the comma who would have been counted as a letter.) This practice satisfied him only until he found himself developing the skill of being able to estimate the number of letters in phrases of several words even while he was composing them.

It was a fateful day, so the game-player sometimes says – it was a fateful day, although he has no recollection of it, when he first decided that the only set of words suitable for deciding the outcomes of his image-events was the sentence, and not the simple sentence with a subject and a predicate but the complex sentence with at least two subordinate clauses. He could not possibly estimate in advance the number of letters in such a sentence, so he supposed, and he was right. Like the words and phrases that he had previously used, the complex sentences had as their subject-matter the persons, places, and events of the fantasy itself – I mean, of course, the images of such things. So, he might compose, in order to decide the outcome needed in the earlier example, a sentence such as *He approved of the style of her brief bathing-costume, which was pale green and contrasted oddly with her bare, sunburned shoulders.*

At some point during the developments reported in the previous paragraph, the game-player made a decision that seems to him now to have been inevitable but was slow to occur to him.

He decided that the number of possible outcomes for every event should be not two but five. His having only two possible outcomes resulted often in his female characters, so to call them, displaying a not-to-be-believed fickleness. Sometimes he was stimulated by the unpredictability of one or another female, but mostly he was not only baffled and annoyed by her seeming changes of moods but hard pressed to devise new ways for his imagined self to approach her without turning his fantasy into farce. And so, on another fateful but unremembered day, he decided that each possible event should admit of five possible outcomes: one extremely favourable; one moderately so; one neutral; one moderately unfavourable; and one extremely so. His offering, on the beach, to kiss a female personage would have five possible outcomes ranging from her falling into his arms to her slapping his face. Of course, he now had to count by fives in his sentences, which made any sort of cheating quite impossible.

His imagined adventures had become by now much more satisfying but also much more drawn out, sometimes so much so that he was apt to forget, on some or another day in the real world, so to call it, what he had decided, on the previous day, were the latest happenings, so to call them, in the other. And so, on an even more fateful day than the earlier two, as he says, he began to record in writing what he likes to call his image-imaginings. From this he needed to take one small step towards the final, perfect modification of his game. He made it a rule that each sentence of his text would not only record the latest seeming-event in the game but would, at the same time, determine details of the event following. While he was composing some or another complex sentence to report the chief character's offering to kiss some or another female character, he was, at the same time, deciding what would be the result of his so offering and the series of events that would afterwards follow. The game, it might be said, determined its own course; the text, it might be said, wrote itself.

We others have mixed reactions to all of this. Some of us consider horse-racing games or games indulging sexual fantasies or any other such enterprises as wasters of the time and the mental energy that ought to be devoted to the writing of fiction. Others see the games as harmless recreation or even as a sort of training for the task of fiction-writing. One of us even considers these and all other such games as being themselves an esoteric sort of fiction. A few of us have been allowed to look into some of the series of labelled folders containing reports of the second sort of game and have reported as follows.

The account of each game consists of no fewer than a hundred handwritten pages and often of many more. Many a game has for its chief characters what seems to be a fictional version of the author of the game as a young man, hardly more than a boy, and one or more dark-haired young women, hardly more than girls, who are his cousins. Many a game ends with the humiliation of the chief male character by one or more cousin or with his being punished by one or more of their mothers, the dark-haired sisters of his own mother. The actual sentences reporting the games are faultless in shape but often contain words and phrases used often by the writers of what is commonly called romantic fiction. (Somewhere in this building is a colony of writers of this sort of fiction, although none of us has sought to learn where.) The author of the reports declines to answer questions about this last matter, and we are, as usual, divided in our opinions, some of us believing the passages in question to be mere parody and asserting that a place might well be found in some or another work of serious fiction for a summary, at least, of the sort of imagined events so to call them, that end sometimes with a scene, so to call it, in which a stern-faced woman throws a jug of ice-water into the groin of a young man, hardly more than a boy, who has exposed himself to a dark-haired young woman, hardly more than a girl, his cousin and the woman's daughter.

While I was standing at my window early this morning and trying not to put off for too much longer the moment when I would sit yet again at my desk and would wait yet again for my first glimpse of the possible subject-matter of the first sentence that I would struggle to write, I saw far off in the mostly level landscape surrounding this house in every direction a flash of sunlight on what was surely the windscreen of a car or a truck passing along one or another of the back roads of this district. A farmer, perhaps, was driving himself and his dogs to an outlying paddock.

On many another morning, I would have wanted, even if briefly, to have been the driver behind that flashing windscreen. I would have wanted to have business other than the writing of fiction; to live among persons who read fiction hardly ever or not at all; to consider as my life's work the management of a farm in the sort of mostly level grassy landscape that I see nowadays only in the distance when I look up from my desk and away from the sort of task that might well seem pointless to most of the inhabitants of that landscape. I would not have spurned fiction, I who sat behind a flashing windscreen this morning, far away from a house of two or, perhaps three storeys. Sometimes during an evening, when my other tasks had been finished, I would look into some or another book of fiction borrowed by my wife from the library in the town at the centre of our district. I might not set out to read the whole book; I might well let the book fall open and then begin reading the pages in front of me. However little I read, I would come to admire the achievement, as I saw it, of the author of the book in front of me, who was able to see in mind always the clear and solid details that made up the contents of his or her fiction. In short, I would suppose, wrongly, of course, that an author of fiction has always available an ample supply of – what shall I call them? – characters, plots, and dialogue in a storage-place called the imagination.

When I stood at the window this morning, I was trying to keep in mind the details of a dream that had occurred to me a few hours earlier, while I was asleep on my folding bed in a corner of this room. I had dreamed that I was conversing at length with a dark-haired and utterly unattractive woman in late middle-age. (I myself am past middle-age, but in the dream I felt myself to be a young man, hardly more than a boy.) At some point during my conversation with the dark-haired woman, my mother, herself dark-haired and past middle-age, appeared, as personages appear in dreams, and asked me the name of the dark-haired woman. The woman had not told me her name but I knew, as one knows things in dreams, that her name was Wilma, which happens to be a name that I dislike. My mother then asked me what was going on, as she put it, between myself and Wilma. It never occurred to my dreaming self to ask my mother by what right she had asked such a question of me. I simply denied to my mother that anything was going on, which was as true as any detail of a dream might be said to be true.

There was much more to the dream, so much more that I spent most of the morning trying to find connections between the subject-matter of the dream and what might be called the underlying meaning of this work of fiction. Then, at lunchtime, I told the others a little about my dream and I tried to introduce into the slight-seeming discussion taking place in the common-room in this corridor these two questions: what differences, if any, may be said to exist between personages such as her whom I named Wilma and those personages who appear to us often while we write? And, if any such differences may be said to exist, must we conclude that the two sorts of personages have their origins in two separate places?

I had expected some of those in the room to be annoyed by my questions, but I was hardly prepared for what took place. One of them set up at once a certain catchcry and moved towards the door. The others, every one of them, took up the catchcry and picked up their sandwiches and pies and pasties and apples and bananas and moved to follow the first man. *Describe a dream – lose a reader!* was their cry, and I was all the more annoyed because I recalled having passed on to them those very words long before, when I was telling them some of the advice that I had read many years before in books published in the USA for the guidance of teachers and students of creative writing, so to call it.

They brought their lunches back to the table after I had promised to say no more about my dream or about my interest in the possible connections between what we dream while asleep and what we see in mind while we write fiction. I supposed that my having mentioned my mother or, I should say, a dream-image of my mother, had caused them to believe I had gone over to the enemy: that I had become some sort of follower of the twentieth-century theorists who had seemed to their followers to have explained the workings of the mind, as though a leaning blade of grass might have found itself capable of explaining the source and the destination of the wind that overpowers it. No one was less likely than I to accept any theory of the mind, and I wish that my colleagues had heard me out and had offered comments after I had been able to tell them that Wilma, so to call her, had later, in reply to my asking her, as I often ask strangers in order to start a conversation, where she came from, had told me that she had grown up in *Gormenghast*, which is the title of a work of fiction that I read more than forty years ago and have quite forgotten except for the detail that the setting, so to call it, of the work is a building many times more vast than this.

Reader, whether you discern or struggle to discern, you should hardly be aggrieved to learn that the writer of this and the following paragraphs is not an occupant, even for the time being, of any visible building of two or, perhaps, three storeys but rather a man past middle-age and older by several years than was the writer who was mentioned much earlier in this work as having been run down and killed while walking home drunkenly of an evening in a certain provincial city of this state. I am like the other writer in that I moved, late in life, away from the capital city of this state. He moved to a large provincial city in the near-west. I moved to a small township in the far west. In the city whither he had moved, many a building is of two or, perhaps, three storeys, which suggests that he may well have seen, while he walked drunkenly homewards on many an evening, one or more windows looking like drops of golden oil, after which he might have concluded that if he were to be run down a few moments later and were to lie dying on the roadside, he could take satisfaction from his perceiving that his life had been all of a piece.

In the small township whither I moved late in life, no house is of more than one storey. We have grain-silos at the edge of the township and a water-tower near the main street, but whenever I walk home drunkenly I see around me nothing resembling a drop of golden oil. I am aware, however, that the township is surrounded on all sides by mostly level grassy countryside. Every street in the township ends at a view of sheep paddocks or croplands. The butterflies reported earlier as passing through

Casterbridge might not even perceive any change in their surroundings if they were to flit over our few streets, where the silence is so profound that the sound of a single motor vehicle can be heard from far away, even by a drunken person. And even if, while I stride homewards with the faintly comical precision of a drunkard, some vehicle should unaccountably appear in my path and should run me down, then I would lie dying with the same equanimity that may have possessed the other writer. Around him, in the towering buildings erected by those grown wealthy from mining, the golden windows would have reminded him of his autobiography, long since published and acclaimed. Around me would appear not actual sights but images of a desk and a bookshelf and a window that I could not doubt had appeared sometimes to a distant observer as a drop of golden oil.

Whenever we learn that one of us is drawing up plans or making notes for a wholly new piece of fiction, we assume, unless the plan-drawer and note-maker has told us otherwise, that his deciding on a new work has come about not as a result of his feeling as though he is in possession of an abundant or overflowing quantity of knowledge but from quite the opposite – from his feeling that he knows too little about a certain subject and ought to know much more. The phrase *a certain subject* in the previous sentence might suggest that what provokes the author is the sort of thing that might provoke a philosopher or a psychologist or a so-called social scientist to embark on a so-called research project, but our sort of author has little in common with those sorts of investigators. He, our author, is likely to be aware of no more than a few clustered images or even of one image. Sometimes, the image may be complex and may seem to yield some of its meaning almost at first sight, as, for example, an image of a castle with each room occupied by a character from some or another film; sometimes, the image may be simple and may seem to be of scant meaning as, for example, an image of a window-pane coloured gold by the afternoon sunlight. Whatever sort of image the author has in mind, he feels a certain feeling seeming to emanate from the image. The feeling is persistent, intense, and sometimes troubling, and yet, at the same time, promising. When the author first becomes aware of this feeling, he might seem to receive the same sort of wordless message that sometimes reaches him from some or another image-person or image-object in some or another dream. He seems to receive wordlessly the message: *Write about me in order to discover my secret and to learn what a throng of images, as yet invisible, lie around me.* (Is even the least discerning reader surprised to learn how different are our methods from those of the numerous group that we call, contemptuously, the paraphrasers of yesterday's newspaper headlines: those who write, often with what is praised as moral indignation or incisive social commentary, about matters that none of us in this building has ever understood, let alone wanted to comment on?)

And so, in time, the writer begins to write, but not before he has given thought to the question what form of narration he had best employ. The author whose deciding to write a wholly new piece of fiction is, for the time being, my own subject-matter has chosen, let us suppose, the very method of narration that I would have chosen in his circumstances, which is the same method of narration that I have used throughout the work of fiction of thirty-four sections of which this it the thirty-first section. The author has chosen to report in the third person and in the past tense the thoughts and deeds of a chief character while reserving the right to comment in the first person if the need arises. As confusing as it may seem to an undiscerning reader, I have to remind every sort of reader that an author who chooses thus to report is not merely choosing a certain form of narration but is casting himself in the role of a certain sort of personage.

The author who was mentioned early in the previous paragraph and will be called henceforth the narrator begins his task by reporting that a certain man who will be called henceforth the chief character has been troubled, at different periods of his life, by images of certain details of a certain forest that he visited several times as a child. The chief character, who is himself an author of fiction, wrote, twenty years before, a piece of fiction in which the same forest was mentioned often. After he had written the fiction, which was later published, he supposed that he would never again be troubled by images of certain details of the forest, one margin of which was sometimes visible from the district of mostly level grassy countryside where he had lived for several years as a child. (Almost all of the forest was destroyed more than fifty years ago, and the land that had once been covered by forest was turned into dairy farms and roads and townships, but that was not the reason for the man's supposing what he supposed. The man was *more* likely to be troubled by images of things if they were no longer visible.) In recent years, however, the man was troubled by images of certain forest plants that he had handled as a child and of a certain bird that he had seen as a child when it flew across a clearing in the forest. These were some of the same images that had caused him, twenty years before, to write passages of fiction for which the setting, so to call it, is the forest, but the images troubled him, on the later occasion, differently, as though the meaning that they yielded earlier was by no means all of the meaning that they were capable of yielding.

One evening during his early childhood, he had played at the edge of the forest with his cousins, the sons and daughters of an older sister of his mother. This woman and her husband and children lived in a clearing in the forest. He and his cousins had chased one another and had hidden from one another at the edges of the clearing, but he had run further into the forest than had they and had hidden there and had not been found but had given himself up when the game had ended. He was not afraid of the forest. He thought of forests, and especially of clearings in forests, as places of refuge and of safety. While he had run from his cousins, he had clutched or had tugged at several sorts of forest plant. The spike-like foliage of one sort of plant had pricked his palms whenever he clutched at it, and the sharp-edged leaves of another plant had cut into the skin of his fingers and had drawn blood whenever he had let the leaves run through his hands. His memory of these simple-seeming events and of the sight reported in the following paragraph were all that urged him to write, but their urging was insistent.

On a certain afternoon in summer, perhaps even earlier than the evening mentioned above, he had been with his father in a clearing in a dense part of the forest. His father was felling trees to be stored and dried for firewood. A brightly coloured bird flew across the clearing, and at one point in its flight the sunlight seemed to flash from the bird's plumage. Long afterwards, and long after the forest had been mostly destroyed, he still recalled the seeming flash of sunlight on the feathers of the bird which was a sacred kingfisher, so his father had said. The predominant colours of the bird were royal blue and a colour that might have been cream or white but had seemed, when the sunlight flashed on it, silver-grey.

I have mentioned already in these paragraphs the feeling that seems to emanate from certain image-objects. I ought to mention also the counter-feeling, so to call it, with which the intending author must respond if his work of fiction is to be written. Despite his having, in the beginning, a few mental images and intimations, the author, by going on with his writing, declares his confidence in these sparse signs and in the many-faceted whole that surely has them at its visible junctures. To use the example of the author mentioned in these paragraphs, I might declare that his setting out to write as he does is a demonstration of his trust in the forest or, rather, the image-forest.

Trust in imagery can serve a writer well, but quite another sort of trust is often needed to sustain a writer of fiction, especially the sort who make up our little band. Admittedly, one or two of us claim hardly to think of their readers but to draw inspiration from the task itself: to keep often in mind the splendid intricacy of the finished text and even to feel, as they complete page after page, that their writing expands their sense of who they are and of how much meaning can be found in a few meagre-seeming experiences. We are more likely, though, when we discuss the matter, to confess that each of us develops while he writes an image of a personage deserving to be called the implied reader. We are sometimes surprised to be reminded by one another that this personage is seldom of the sort whose name appears often in the dedication of a book; is seldom a parent or a wife or a child. The personage, so to call her – and we, being males, make her out almost always to be female – is someone scarcely known to us. For a few of us, she is by definition always unknowable except for the one fact that she will one day read our words with discernment. Some see her image clearly and can report such details as the colour of her hair; others sense her only as a presence unlikely ever to reveal herself to their inner eye, so to call it. All of us agree on two matters. First, we have no wish to meet up with her; our being able to write as we do depends on our never so meeting. Even were we to hear it rumoured that this house accommodates not only a hundred kinds of writer but numbers of kinds of what might be called writerly persons including, in some remote corridor of the farthest wing from here, a few females admirably qualified to serve as ghostly but discerning readers of texts still in the writing – even then, none of us would go any way towards seeking out those few and would surely be even more careful afterwards to avoid the groups of female persons sometimes seen strolling in the grounds around this wing.

The second matter on which we all agree is that our implied readers are utterly to be trusted.

The following paragraphs will report much of what will surely go into the making of the piece of fiction the beginnings of which were reported in the section before the previous section.

The chief character had never learned the correct sequence of the places where his mother had lived before her marriage. He knew that she had been born in a small town on the plains that occupy much of the south-west of his and her native state and that her father had died before her birth. He knew that she and his father had been living in rented rooms in a western suburb of the capital city when he, their eldest child, had been born. At some time during the eighteen years between, she had lived at several addresses in the largest provincial city in the south-west of the state; she had even lived at some time in the largest forest in the south-west, a forest that was later destroyed almost wholly. She was the youngest of nine siblings, most of them females, and by the time when she was aged in her teens, most of the siblings had left home.

At some time early in his mother's childhood, her widowed mother had remarried. Her new husband was a man who had been previously unmarried. The chief character had often, as a child, been taken to visit this man and his wife and had called him, for convenience, Grandfather although his, the child's mother, had explained that the man was not his true grandfather. He, the child, had neither liked nor disliked the man, although the child's mother had told the child that the man had often been drunk in earlier times and had sometimes locked her and the younger of her siblings out of their house and had threatened them with violence.

All except two of the persons mentioned in the previous three paragraphs were long dead when the chief character was visited by a man from a far northern state who told him that they two were half-brothers. The man from the north had with him papers proving that he and the chief character had had the same mother. They had been born in different hospitals in the same capital city, the man from the north about a year before the chief character. The man from the north had been placed in the care of a so-called babies' home a week after his birth. He had later been adopted and had been given the surname of his adopting parents. He had been told as a young man that he had been adopted but had not been able until many years later to learn the name of his mother. After having learned her name, he went to much trouble to discover her address, which was in the south-western provincial city mentioned earlier. He then wrote to her, asking politely whether she could help in his search for his true mother. She, his true mother, had a solicitor write a letter beneath his letterhead telling the man from the north that she was unable to help him in his search and warning him that if he tried again to make contact with her she would take legal action against him. After he had received this letter, the man from the north had had what he described to his half-brother as a nervous breakdown.

The chief character had felt sorry for the man from the north and had answered patiently the many questions that he asked about their mother. One of the few questions that the chief character could not answer was the question why their mother had repudiated her eldest son.

The man from the north was, of course, curious as to who had been his father. He showed the chief character a copy of his, the older man's birth certificate. The father was named by his surname only. The surname told the chief character nothing.

After his half-brother had gone back to the north, the chief character visited the other of the two surviving persons mentioned above. This was a woman aged in her nineties and the last survivor of his mother's siblings. She had left her family home before the time when the half-brother, so to call him, would have been conceived and she had not learned of his existence until some years later, but she was willing to tell what she knew. She claimed that the father of the child had not been the person named as the father on the birth certificate.

According to the surviving sister, her youngest sister had been living, at the time when she conceived, with her mother and her stepfather on a small farm, a so-called soldier-settler's block, far inside the forest mentioned often in previous paragraphs. The youngest sister was the only one of the nine siblings who had not already left home. Several of the younger girls had left home in order to avoid their stepfather, who had sometimes exposed himself to them and had seemed often likely to make sexual advances to them. The surviving sister had no doubt that the father of her youngest sister's first child was her stepfather. The surname identifying the child's father on the birth certificate was the surname of a young man, hardly more than a boy, who had sometimes done labouring work for the stepfather, and the survivor believed that her youngest sister had been induced to name him as the father in order to conceal the true identity of the father. The person who had induced her, according to the surviving sister, was her mother.

The surviving sister spoke harshly of the mother, who had been, of course, her own mother. The survivor claimed that the mother had known why the younger sisters had left home but had pretended not to know. The survivor even claimed to remember the circumstances that led to her younger sister's conceiving her first child. She, the survivor, had visited her mother regularly after having left home and had learned during one of her visits that the mother intended to be away from home for several days while she visited her own mother, who lived in a small town on the plains that occupy much of the south-west of the state where these events are reported to have taken place. The chief character had concluded from this last piece of information that his mother as a young woman had not been able to trust her own mother or, that if she had trusted her mother, the trust had been misplaced.

A well-known writer of fiction in this country, once, as part of a discussion about one of his books, which could fairly be called a work of historical fiction, said or, perhaps, wrote words to the effect that he insisted on his right to imagine the past. I have often wondered at his statement. If I assume that he was not making the preposterous claim that he was somehow better qualified than other living persons to suppose what one or another person thought or felt, say, a hundred years ago, then what was he claiming? Perhaps his emphasis was on the word *imagining*, as though he had other means at his disposal for discovering what this or that person felt a hundred years ago but chose to use his imagination. And yet, what other means could he or anyone possibly call on for such a task?

Reader, we are all of us, whether writers or readers, surely obliged to imagine the past, although I, who dislike the word *imagine*, would prefer to use such an expression as *speculate about*. And surely each of us in this wing of this building, given the nature of our subject-matter, so to call it, might be called a writer of historical fiction, if not an interpreter of history. A certain one of us might learn, if he so wished, when was built the house of stone where his father's father lived throughout his life and, after him, throughout their lives four of his children, all of them unmarried. Another of us might learn, if he so wished, where stood formerly a certain cottage of timber in a clearing in a forest long since destroyed – the cottage whence his mother's mother once set out to visit her own mother in a township surrounded by mostly level grassy countryside. But in order to learn what we most desire to learn about the persons in that house or that cottage, we would have to be enabled to be readers of works of fiction with those persons for their implied authors and with narrators wholly to be trusted: works of fiction which drew, perhaps, on the experience of their authors.

The narrator of this present work of fiction is unable to end the work other than by reporting of the chief character of the work of fiction mentioned often in the final pages of this work that he seems only to see and to feel when he might have been expected to speculate and to imagine. He seems to see the flashing of sunlight on the blue and silver-grey plumage of a bird and he seems to feel a prickling in his hands from certain foliage and a pain in his fingers after certain sharp-sided leaves had drawn blood.

The single holland blind in his room is still drawn down, even though the time is early evening and a traveller looking hither from far away in the mostly level grassy countryside surrounding this building might see the window as a drop of golden oil among sumless such drops. I walked in the grounds a short while ago and looked up at his room. (We know better than to knock at his door.) I looked up and saw a dull pane of glass rather than a drop of golden oil. I saw a window and behind it a drawn blind. In short, I learned nothing. But what could I have been hoping to learn about the flesh-and-blood author, the breathing author of these and who knows how many other pages of true fiction?

This project has been assisted by the Commonwealth Government through the Australia Council, its arts funding and advisory body.